THEY CAME TO SONORA

Dean Stratemeyer—The tough, impossible-to-shake operative who swore he would end the Sonora Kid's reign of terror.

Sharon Cortland—From the family farm in Maine she tracked her brother, hoping against hope he had not been brutally murdered in the mad rush for California gold.

Dan Prentiss—He sought his fortune as a prospector but soon staked his claim on a future with Sharon—if her quest didn't get them both killed.

Rafe Barnett—Once the miners of Sonora committed a violent outrage against him and his young wife. Now he has returned with a ruthless secret plan to exact his revenge.

The Stagecoach Series
Ask your bookseller for the books you have missed

STAGECOACH STATION 9:
SONORA

Hank Mitchum

Created by the producers of
Wagons West, White Indian,
Saga of the Southwest, and
The Kent Family Chronicles Series.

Executive Producer: Lyle Kenyon Engel

BANTAM BOOKS
TORONTO · NEW YORK · LONDON · SYDNEY

STAGECOACH STATION 9: SONORA

*A Bantam Book / published by arrangement with
Book Creations, Inc.*

Bantam edition / December 1983

Produced by Book Creations, Inc.
Executive Producer: Lyle Kenyon Engel.

ISBN 0-553-23723-3

Published simultaneously in the United States and Canada

*Bantam Books are published by Bantam Books, Inc. Its trademark,
consisting of the words "Bantam Books" and the portrayal of a
rooster, is Registered in U.S. Patent and Trademark Office and in
other countries. Marca Registrada. Bantam Books, Inc., 666 Fifth
Avenue, New York, New York 10103.*

PRINTED IN THE UNITED STATES OF AMERICA

H   0 9 8 7 6 5 4 3 2 1

STAGECOACH STATION 9:

SONORA

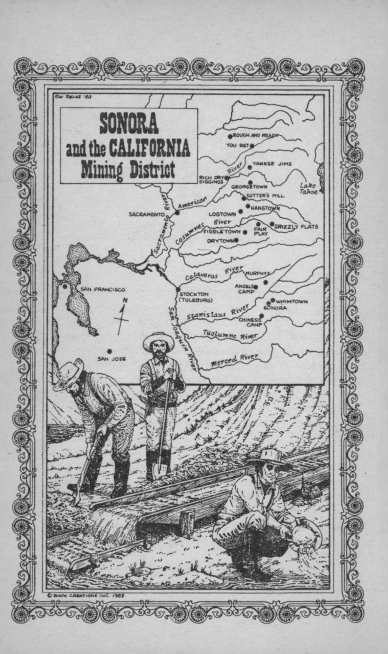

SONORA
and the CALIFORNIA
Mining District

ROUGH AND READY
YOU BET
YANKEE JIMS
RICH DRY DIGGINGS
GEORGETOWN
SUTTER'S MILL
Lake Tahoe
SACRAMENTO
American River
Sacramento River
LOGTOWN
River
HANGTOWN
Cosumnes
FIDDLETOWN
FAIR PLAY
GRIZZLY FLATS
DRYTOWN
Calaveras River
MURPHYS
SAN FRANCISCO
STOCKTON
(TULEBURG)
ANGELS CAMP
San Joaquin River
Stanislaus River
WHIMTOWN
SONORA
CHINESE CAMP
Tuolumne River
SAN JOSE
Merced River

© BOOK CREATIONS INC. 1983

July 1850

Rafael Escobar wanted to believe it was only a fearsome nightmare. But the harsh voices around him were too loud, the distorted faces crowding upon him too vivid to be contained within the fragile confines of a dream. The monstrous shadows were filled with solid beings—the stench of whiskey emanating from their shouting mouths was as real as the heaving of his own stomach.

Now, as he saw Josita being pushed roughly through the crowd, he knew this was really happening. These demented gringos were actually going to hang his wife!

"Stop!" he screamed. "You cannot do this!"

He tore himself away from the two men at his side and plunged through the crowd after Josita. Hands grabbed at him, but not until he reached the saloon's porch was he finally restrained. While he continued to struggle, Colonel Hiram B. Polk bellied his way through the ranks of drink-sodden miners and leaned close to advise him. It was he who had acted as judge throughout the fifteen-minute travesty of a trial.

"My dear sir," Polk declared, "you must realize how this pains me. All of us. But justice must be done! Your

1

woman has murdered a white man. Stabbed him to death! Everyone admits this. Your wife admits it!"

"She was fighting Bullock off!" Rafael screamed. "You heard her. He was in there with her. He was drunk! He broke in!"

"Saving her honor was she?"

"Yes! Damn you! Yes!"

Laughter erupted from all sides. The colonel straightened and glanced around knowingly at the grinning miners. Then with a broad wink at them, he looked back down at Rafael.

"But my dear sir, that is out of the question," the colonel said, grinning slyly. "A Mexican whore has no honor to protect."

Screaming with rage, Rafael broke free of his captors and hurled himself at the colonel. Grabbing for Polk's throat, Rafael bore the colonel down beneath him, his fingers tightening convulsively. The colonel, gasping, began to claw frantically at the hands gripping him, but before Rafael could choke out his life, a stunning blow on the back of the head rendered Rafael nearly senseless.

He rolled off the colonel. At once Rafael felt himself being kicked brutally by a swarming crowd of outraged miners. His attackers went at it with such enthusiasm Rafael could hear their breathing become labored. Only dimly was he aware of the colonel's voice urging the miners to cease. "After all," the colonel reminded them, "Escobar is the whore's husband. He has a right to be upset."

Still panting like wild animals, the miners pulled back from him. Rough hands pulled Rafael to a sitting position and trussed his wrists behind his back. Someone else slapped him brutally in the face to bring him around. His head pounding horribly, Rafael opened his eyes and saw Bill Finney leaning close. On more than one occasion had Rafael and his wife dealt with Finney, and the fellow had seemed reasonable enough for a gringo—at times, even pleasant.

Yet now he was a member of this lynch mob!

Losing interest in Rafael, the crowd rushed off the porch to surge around a flatbed wagon just pulling up. It was Jim Coleman's wagon, drawn by two horses. Coleman pulled the team to a halt, then waited as the hangman climbed up onto the wagon and flung his rope over a tree limb.

Josita appeared then, walking steadily with head erect through the crowd of miners toward the wagon. Tears of frustration and rage nearly blinded Rafael upon seeing her. He tried to pull free of the rope that bound him and found that his arms had no strength left. He wanted to cry out, but even that was impossible. The blow on the back of his head seemed to have struck him dumb. All he could do was watch in horror as the miners—suddenly quieting—moved back, allowing Josita the room she needed to clamber calmly up onto the tailgate beside the hangman.

She paused to brush off her skirt as soon as she was standing upright, a radiantly beautiful woman with long tresses as dark as midnight and eyes so luminous they rivaled the stars. There was nothing Rafael could do. They were going to hang her!

Josita gazed down at the crowd and asked for a belt or a piece of rope. One of the miners handed up his belt to her. She fastened it around her skirts to prevent them from billowing up immodestly. Then she took the noose from the hangman and placed it around her neck, bending her head back slightly in order to tighten it more securely. At the same time she was careful to see to it that her long hair hung outside the rope. These details attended to, she said something to the hangman, who promptly jumped off the wagon.

Looking down at the hushed crowd, Josita smiled. It was a proud, imperious smile. "*Adiós, señores!*" she said.

With hands folded decorously before her, she turned and nodded to Coleman. His whip cracked. The horses sprang forward. A collective sigh escaped the crowd.

Something deep within Rafael's soul crumbled. He sagged to the floor of the porch, unconscious.

Chapter 1

In the summer of 1852, a stagecoach labored up the steep grade paralleling the Stanislaus River. Six hours out of Stockton, the stagecoach was heading for the town of Sonora, prospering headquarters for the placer mining still flushing gold from the hills and streams of California.

The legend inscribed in red and gold letters on the mud-splattered side panels of the Concord coach read The Sonora Stage and Hauling Company. The fine, handsome stagecoach, recently delivered from the East, rocked securely on its leather thoroughbraces. Built by the famous Abbott and Downing Coach and Wagon Manufacturers of Concord, New Hampshire, it was easily a match for the treacherous and rutted road it was forced to negotiate as it wound ever higher into the foothills of the Sierra Nevada.

The driver was a burly, red-faced Scotsman in his early forties, with a mass of unruly hair spilling out from under his battered derby. As the grade grew steeper, he jumped to his feet. Hurling oaths that approached poetry in their awesome implications, he sent his whip snaking out over the heaving backs of his six horses. Again and again its crack echoed so loudly it cut sharply through the thundering rattle of the coach. When the coach reached the crest at last, the driver slumped back down onto the seat and put aside his whip. He propped his foot lightly against the brake, taking advantage of this momentary lull to hand the reins to his shotgun messenger and reach for the silver whiskey flask tucked into his belt.

The lean, berry-brown young man of twenty sitting beside him grinned as he took the reins and watched the driver tip his flask high. It was always a delight to hear the Scot cuss his team with such lordly abandon. Stoppering the flask, the driver took the ribbons back from the shotgun messenger, who then took up his double-barreled shotgun and glanced around at the steep-sided flanks now beginning to close in on the narrow roadway.

The Sonora Kid had not robbed this stage line for better than a month now, but as the driver had remarked to him when they pulled out of Stockton, on this trip they were transporting enough gold to tempt a saint.

And the Sonora Kid was no saint.

There were five passengers inside the stage. Each of them was glad that the long pull up the steep grade was over—the two women, especially. Try as they might, it had been impossible for Sharon Cortland and Belle Harper not to hear generous portions of the driver's colorful language. By the time the ridge had been reached, both women's faces were unnaturally pink, and they were doing their best to avoid the eyes of the male passengers.

Settling back in her seat, Sharon turned her gaze out the side window at the rugged wilderness and was soon lost in her own anxious thoughts. This steep, craggy country was certainly different from the interminable ocean she had been forced to gaze upon for close to five months during her passage around South America.

Not that the entire trip had been boring and uneventful. Far from it. Their fool of a captain had decided at the last moment to attempt that particularly barbarous passage through the Straits of Magellan. That their flimsy matchbox of a bark had not been smashed to kindling against the rocks or that all of them had not been swept overboard was to her way of thinking a miracle, plain and simple.

A pretty, vivacious blonde of twenty-two with a wide, expressive mouth and astonishingly blue eyes, Sharon had left her home on a farm near Portland, Maine, to search for her brother, Tim, who was a year younger than she. A little more than a year before, Tim had left for the goldfields of California.

Soon after Tim's departure, many of the prospectors had begun trickling home from California, bringing back with them little gold but many heart-rending stories of disease and deprivation—enough to alarm even the most sanguine, Sharon and her family included. Then had come a single letter from Tim, containing anything but comforting news. Tim was sick with the cholera. At once Sharon told her family she would journey to California and retrieve Tim and return him to the bosom of his family. He was worth more—far more—than any gold he could possibly claw out of such a wild, inhospitable land.

She turned her gaze from the window. From her bosom she plucked a well-worn envelope and extracted from it her brother's letter. Soon she was caught up again in Tim's excitement at finally having reached the placer streams. True to his gallant nature, only at the very last had he admitted to coming down with the cholera. Folding the letter, Sharon put it back in its envelope and sighed. No matter how often she read Tim's words, she always felt the same awful dread at his mention of that scourge, cholera. Recently it had swept through the southern states, and rumors of its awesome virulence had spread through New England with the speed that always accompanies disaster.

Sharon returned the letter to her bosom and directed her gaze once more out the stage window. She must force herself to have positive thoughts, she told herself firmly. She had not come all this way to be disappointed. She was sure that Tim would be alive and well and would welcome her with open arms, a broad smile on his dear, familiar face. She took a deep breath and smiled. Yes, that was how it would be.

Directly across from Sharon sat a young man whose

pulse was racing. A moment before, while the driver was cursing at the horses, Dan Prentiss had seen the flush growing in Sharon's cheeks and had wanted to lean over and comfort her. But his courage had betrayed him, leaving him frozen in place, his tongue unable to function. Indeed, from the moment Sharon Cortland stepped aboard the stage in Stockton and introduced herself, he had been struck dumb by her golden beauty.

A tall, broad-shouldered man in his early twenties with hair the color of burnished copper, Dan filled out his expensive clothes impressively. His eyes were gray and friendly. Had he not been so intimidated by Sharon's beauty, he would have long since shared with her the mounting excitement he felt—his eager optimism as he approached the fabled goldfields of California.

He knew, of course, that much of the gold had already been gleaned from California's streams, but Dan Prentiss was certain more remained, and he meant to get his share. From what he had heard in San Francisco, the mother-lode country north of Sonora would be the best place for him to start.

Dan had prepared himself well for his great quest. While working as a manager of a gentlemen's clothing store in New York City, he had saved almost six hundred dollars. With this sum in hand, he had abandoned his tedious job and booked passage to California via the Isthmus of Panama, the crossing of which having been an adventure he would savor for the rest of his life.

Now on the last leg of his journey, he still had five hundred dollars in treasury bills in his pocket, a sum he was sure would be enough to outfit him for his new role. Though he had been warned about the inflated prices in San Francisco and Stockton, they had still astonished him mightily. He was hoping that conditions would be a little more sensible farther inland. If not, a secondhand pick and shovel, not to mention rockers or pans, would be just as valuable to him as newly minted versions. Dan reasoned that among the disgruntled miners quitting the diggings every day, there was sure to be one who would place little value on his tools and equipment—now just impediments to his flight back home.

Dan's musings were halted abruptly when Sharon Cortland turned from the window. Their eyes met. She had such incredibly blue eyes. The glance lasted only a moment, but Dan almost drowned in their depths. Sharon smiled slightly—almost shyly—at him, then turned her head further to say something to the woman sitting beside her.

Dan looked quickly out the stage window but was oblivious to the spectacular landscape. He was thinking of Sharon, hoping against hope that her smile—no matter how slight—meant something. But even if it did, he chided himself, what did that matter? He was, after all, a grown man. How ridiculous that he should respond in such fashion to a single passing glance—a barely perceptible, fleeting smile. Even more crucial, were she to view him as an easily smitten, callow youth, it would certainly do nothing to advance his cause.

His cause?

In that instant, Dan Prentiss realized that Sharon Cortland had become one of the most important reasons he had for succeeding in his quest for gold.

Dean Stratemeyer—a powerful, heavyset fellow in a brown, rumpled suit and a gray hat—was sitting between Dan Prentiss and the lean, dark-visaged fellow who had climbed aboard the stage in Stockton. The glance that had just passed between Sharon and Dan had not gone unnoticed by him. It amused and gratified him to see how alive Prentiss was to the appeal of a woman as undeniably beautiful as Miss Sharon Cortland.

For his part, Stratemeyer was a little concerned about this lovely young woman, who seemed totally unaware of what a sensation her appearance in a rude mining community would soon cause. Though most of the men would probably treat her with elaborate respect, there were sure to be others not so kind.

Perhaps Belle Harper, the older woman sitting beside

Sharon, would take the younger woman in hand and provide her with some protection, Stratemeyer was thinking. But he realized this was a forlorn hope, at best. Belle's dress and manner did little to disguise the robust fullness of her breasts, and the amount of rouge she had so expertly applied to her round, pleasing features made it pretty clear that her intent was to attract as many honeybees as possible to her fading blossoms. This was her last hurrah, and she would be too busy looking out for herself to spend much time protecting the younger one.

Stratemeyer wished the women luck, even as he washed his hands of any involvement in their affairs. Once he arrived in Sonora his companions in this stagecoach would pass out of his ken. He had other business to tend to—desperate business.

The Sonora Kid had been plundering the Sonora Stage and Hauling Company since its inception less than a year ago. Allan Pinkerton—founder of a fledgling detective agency in Chicago—had sent Stratemeyer to apprehend the notorious highwayman in response to a plea from Bill Finney, the owner of the stage line.

Until Pinkerton personally recruited him for the assignment, Stratemeyer had been a member of the Chicago Police Department. His record in apprehending the murderers and assorted felons and footpads that abounded in the crowded streets and back alleys of the booming city was an enviable one. It was this success that had caused Pinkerton to single him out.

A great deal of Stratemeyer's success was due to his appearance: He did not look the part of a detective. A balding man in his late thirties with a large, friendly beak of a nose, Stratemeyer gave off such an air of guilelessness that he constantly found himself the recipient of knowing smiles and the butt of gentle pranks. Upon meeting him, many people found themselves eager to confide in this big, floppy bear of a man. But Stratemeyer's harmless innocence was more apparent than real. Indeed, his cynicism was complete. Stratemeyer believed in nothing more firmly than he did in the utter depravity of his fellow men. And in that conviction, he had seldom been disappointed.

The stage took a sudden jolt, causing Stratemeyer to reach up quickly for the leather strap. It had been a rough, miserable passage from New Orleans to California via the Cape, and this final lap of the journey was no less fatiguing. The dimensions of the stage were not kind to a man of his bulk, even though in this case the dark, quiet fellow scrunched into the corner beside him had done his best to give Stratemeyer all the room he possibly could.

Their voices so low that above the constant roar of the stagecoach no one in the passenger compartment could hear them, Sharon Cortland and Belle Harper spoke of their plans. Belle had long since confided to Sharon her purpose in making this arduous journey. Just as Stratemeyer had surmised, she was a widow who was quite determined to shed that lonely appellation.

There were men aplenty in California, each one of them hungry for the love and comfort a woman like Belle could provide. Without apologies to anyone, Belle freely admitted that her ambition was to marry a man not only smart enough to have found the gold lying about in this wild country, but also clever enough to hang on to it. With such a man, Belle would be more than happy to make a partnership. And she would give as good as she got. The love, if it came at all, would have to come later. First things first.

"But surely, Belle," whispered Sharon in some surprise, "you wouldn't marry a man you didn't love."

The sweet, touching innocence of that question almost made Belle laugh aloud. Out of courtesy she only smiled. Leaning closer, she replied softly, "Dearie, love can only grow with respect. I could not and would not marry a man I did not respect. The love, I hope, will come later."

"Then you would marry a man for whom you felt no passion? Only respect?"

Doing her best to keep any mockery out of her voice,

Belle replied firmly, "I leave passion to youth. And with it, I leave also the silly blindness that goes with it—and the inevitable sorrow. I have had enough of both, I am afraid."

Sharon thought a moment, then leaned close to Belle. "I do believe you are right, Belle. But I am afraid it is nearly impossible to find a man one can respect—truly respect. Perhaps that is why we settle for those we can only love."

Patting Sharon on the knee, Belle smiled and nodded emphatically. She could not have put it better herself.

The man who called himself Rafe Barnett watched the two women for a moment longer, then pulled himself closer into the corner of the stage. He was a small-boned, dark-eyed man with features as sharp as a blade. A pencil-thin mustache graced his upper lip, giving his straight line of a mouth a decidedly cruel cast. His unblinking, lidded eyes were as dead as yesterday's hope.

The man sitting beside Rafe—the one who had introduced himself as Dean Stratemeyer—was sitting unpleasantly close. Rafe hated the feel of the gringo's solid thigh rubbing against his, and he hated that gringo smell, compounded of booted, unwashed feet, cigar smoke, and sweat. Rafe tried to sit as far from the gringo as he could, but short of disappearing into the coach's woodwork, he could go no farther.

And perhaps that was just as well, for Rafe would have to keep an eye on Stratemeyer when the time came: The big fellow was packing a Navy Colt revolver in a cross-draw holster under his frock coat. Rafe had no doubt that this was the operative Bill Finney had imported from Chicago to stop the Sonora Kid. But he was not impressed. Stratemeyer was a big, slow-moving hulk of a man who would undoubtedly be no more successful than those other two Bill Finney had called in to save his company.

Still, while Stratemeyer carried that revolver, it would do Rafe no harm to be wary of him—and to warn his partner of Stratemeyer's weapon when the time came.

Pulling himself erect, Rafe glanced out the side window. The stagecoach was picking up speed, which meant it was now on the downgrade to Grover's Flats. Rafe glanced swiftly, almost furtively, at his fellow passengers. They were all busy with their own thoughts, not paying him the slightest attention. That was just the way he wanted it.

The ghost of a smile flickered over his dark, impassive face.

On a crag high above the roadway, a lone rider sitting astride a bay gelding came suddenly alert. Standing in his stirrups, he watched the rooster tail of dust marking the stagecoach's progress as it thundered down the steep grade leading to Grover's Flats.

The rider was dressed in the costume of a Californio, those California-born Mexican-Americans who now found themselves despised and dispossessed in a land that for over a century had been theirs. He was wearing a broad-brimmed sombrero trimmed in gold, tight-fitting black trousers, a white silk shirt, and a black buttonless vest also trimmed with brilliant gold thread.

The young Californio turned his horse and with a casual recklessness galloped down a steep, boulder-strewn trail. Pulling up behind a towering boulder, he took from one of his saddlebags a black silk hood fashioned skillfully from a pillow case. Three holes had been cut out of it, two for the eyes and one for the mouth. As the rattle of the approaching stagecoach grew louder, the Californio removed his sombrero, dropped the mask deftly over his head, adjusted the eye and mouth holes, then put his sombrero back on. Two large Colts were tucked into his belt. He withdrew one of them and inspected it carefully before shoving it back into his belt.

There was a moment more of waiting, and then as the stagecoach swept past, the Sonora Kid spurred his mount out from behind the boulder and galloped after it.

As the shotgun messenger was shifting his shotgun to

his left hand, he caught sight of the Sonora Kid's bay
gelding pulling alongside and found himself staring down
into the yawning muzzle of the Kid's revolver. The young
man tossed his shotgun away at once.

The driver saw the hooded rider at the same time,
and with a fearsome curse hauled back suddenly on his
reins. A moment or two later he had brought his six horses
to a scrambling, bone-rattling halt.

Sharon—pulling herself back up onto her seat—managed to poke her head out of the side window first to see
why they had halted so precipitously. Uttering a cry of
dismay, she pulled her head back in and stared across at
Dan Prentiss.

"There's a man out there on a horse!" she told him
breathlessly. "And I do believe he's robbing the stage!"

Stratemeyer pushed past the small fellow beside him
to look out the stage window, but it was the wrong side
and he could see nothing. As he spun to look out the other
window, his hand reached in under his frock coat for his
big Navy Colt. At that moment the door was pulled open,
and the Sonora Kid stood in the doorway, his menacing
revolver covering them all. In a hard, youthful voice, he
ordered them out.

The passengers scrambled frantically from the stage.
Dan Prentiss piled out first, then reached back to help
Sharon Cortland down. Stratemeyer was shoved roughly
to one side as the fellow beside him shouldered past.
Unwilling to start anything at this juncture for fear of
endangering the two women, Stratemeyer released the
grip on his Colt, stepped down, and assisted Belle Harper
from the stage.

Turning then to face the Sonora Kid, Stratemeyer
glimpsed the strongbox resting on the ground a few feet
behind the notorious outlaw.

"Give me your valuables," the Kid barked, stepping
toward them, brandishing his six-gun as he herded them
back against the stage.

The fellow who had burst out of the stage ahead of
Stratemeyer obediently reached into his inside coat pocket

and handed the Kid a billfold heavy with greenbacks. The Kid took the money and was about to move on when he spied a cord around the man's neck. Reaching out swiftly, he grabbed it and yanked upward, causing a small deerskin pouch heavy with gold dust to bounce out into view. Chuckling, the Kid dropped the pouch into one of the saddlebags draped over his shoulder.

The Sonora Kid stepped in front of Stratemeyer, his weapon resting lightly on the detective's chest. With a barely audible chuckle, he reached under Stratemeyer's frock coat and removed the Navy Colt from its holster. Giving it a quick look, he flung it behind him into the rocks. Then he removed Stratemeyer's billfold, took the folding money from it, and with a slight, ironic nod handed the detective back his empty billfold.

Standing before the two women, the Kid appeared interested only in what jewelry was most obvious. Somewhat roughly, he took a set of earrings from Belle Harper and then reached out for an emerald brooch pinned to Sharon Cortland's dress. But the moment the highwayman's fingers closed around the brooch, Sharon burst into tears, startling the Kid. He pulled his hand back sharply, ripping the gem from Sharon's bosom. At once Dan Prentiss reached over and snatched the piece of jewelry from the Kid's hand.

With a quick, vicious swipe of his gun barrel, the Sonora Kid caught Prentiss on his cheekbone. The blow sent Prentiss rocking back against the coach. Contemptuously, the Kid snatched back the brooch, stuck it and the earrings in his pocket, and then reached into Prentiss's jacket and removed his bulging billfold. As the Kid stuffed its contents into his saddlebag, Prentiss looked on with a dismay that had nothing at all to do with his throbbing face.

The Kid stepped back. *"Gracias, señores, señoritas,"* he told them. "Now get back into the stage! Pronto!" He turned to the driver and the shotgun messenger and with a quick motion of his revolver, directed them up into the box.

As soon as the five passengers were inside and the driver had the reins securely, the Sonora Kid punched two swift shots into the sky. The horses bolted frantically, and in a sudden explosive clatter, the stage was on its way.

Inside the stage, Sharon was weeping softly, her face turned away from the others. Belle, obviously outraged, was staring straight ahead, her round face, despite the rouge, unnaturally pale. Sitting back with his head against the seat cushion, Dan Prentiss had an ugly purple welt growing on his cheekbone—and a dazed look in his eyes. He had lost everything. A moment before he had all the money he needed to stake himself to a fortune. Now he was penniless.

Dean Stratemeyer, however, felt only anger. Leaning his head out the window, he called up to the driver to stop. But the driver—anxious to put distance between himself and the Sonora Kid—could not hear Stratemeyer above the furious din of the stage. Giving up on the driver, Stratemeyer pushed open the door and flung himself from the coach. Landing as lightly as a big cat, he went down for a moment on all fours, then glanced up in time to see the stagecoach disappear around a clump of towering pine. In a moment the sound of its passage had been swallowed by the immense, brooding silence of the California wilderness. Stratemeyer's gray hat had flown off. He retrieved it, then started to trot back along the rutted roadway.

The Sonora Kid had no reason to believe he was in any danger from the passengers, and Stratemeyer was hoping he might still find the highwayman busy unloading the strongbox. He slipped behind the rocks as he approached the point of the holdup and pressed on, moving more cautiously but no less swiftly. As he dodged around the rocks close by the spot where the stagecoach had pulled up, he glimpsed the Sonora Kid aboard his bay, leading a heavily laden packhorse eastward into the hills. The empty strongbox lay abandoned, its lid still gaping.

Waiting until the highwayman was out of sight, Stratemeyer hurried for the area where the Kid had flung his revolver. For a few frantic minutes, he found no trace of his weapon as he grubbed about in the underbrush. He had carefully noted where his weapon had landed, he thought, and when he did not find it immediately, he began to fear that the Kid had taken it. At last, pushing back to regain an upright position, his left foot caught at something.

Looking down, he saw his revolver's grip half buried in the gravel. After plucking the weapon from the ground, he broke it open and blew out the barrel. Swiftly, he removed each round, blew out the chambers, checked the action, and reloaded. He could not, of course, be completely sure of the weapon after the punishment it had just taken, but it was all he had.

Pounding along steadily, Stratemeyer topped a gulley and saw the Sonora Kid riding toward a distant ridge, at least a quarter of a mile farther on. Stratemeyer did not alter his speed; he just doggedly kept going. He was not wearing riding boots, which would have made such a pursuit on foot impossible.

About half an hour later, a weary Stratemeyer heard the sharp, close crack of a gunshot from the heavily wooded ridge just above him. He pulled up, listened for a moment, then continued his climb toward the ridge with renewed urgency.

Bursting over the crest, he pulled up in sudden disarray.

Less than fifteen yards from him—no longer wearing his black hood—the Sonora Kid had just finished transferring the sacks of gold from the padded leather *aparejo* on the back of the packhorse to the pair of saddlebags slung over his gelding's haunches. It was a makeshift arrangement, and glimpsing the body of the packhorse farther down the trail, Stratemeyer knew the reason for it. The packhorse had pulled up lame, and that shot had been the Kid making sure the animal did not follow him.

All this Stratemeyer took in with one swift glance. For a split second the two astonished men stared at each other. Stratemeyer was the first to act. Drawing his six-gun, he flung a quick shot at the Kid. Untouched, the Kid leaped aboard his bay, wheeled, and charged down the trail at full gallop.

Using both hands to steady his aim, Stratemeyer fired again. The round caught the Kid in the back, the force of the slug slamming him forward onto the neck of his mount. It looked for a moment as if he were going to pitch forward out of his saddle, but he managed to right himself and keep going.

A moment later the Sonora Kid cut sharply through a group of massive boulders and vanished from sight—leaving Stratemeyer with no choice but to set off on foot again in pursuit.

Chapter 2

The stage thundered into Sonora later that afternoon. As it rattled down narrow Main Street, the excited driver did not hesitate to broadcast the sensational news of the holdup to the townspeople, who soon began racing along on the sidewalks beside the stage. The news traveled swiftly ahead, and by the time the driver pulled his lathered team to a halt in front of the express office, an excited crowd had gathered.

The driver had difficulty climbing down, so closely did the townspeople press around the stage. Once on the ground, he was immediately surrounded.

"Someone get the sheriff!" he cried.

There was immediate laughter at this, but two men at the rear of the crowd obediently spun around and hurried toward the Gold Nugget.

"Driver!" called Belle Harper, as she climbed out of the coach. "What are you going to do about that passenger who jumped from the stage?"

The driver looked at Belle incredulously as she pushed her way through the crowd toward him. "What's that, ma'am? You say a passenger *jumped* from the stage?"

"You mean you didn't see him?" Belle asked, amazed.

18

"I don't know what in Sam Hill you're talking about, ma'am. You mean someone fell out of the stage?"

"It was Mr. Dean Stratemeyer. And he didn't fall. He jumped!"

A startled murmur swept through the crowd.

"You must be mistaken, ma'am," the driver insisted. "Why in tarnation would anyone want to do a fool thing like that?"

"How do I know?" Belle responded. "If you didn't see one of your own passengers leap from the stage, the rest of us did! Someone must go back and help that poor man!"

The sheriff arrived. He seemed to be moving through a vague, alcoholic fog. He had a broad bovine face with a bulbous nose lit brightly enough to show him his way in the dark. He looked as if he had swollen to twice his size without once changing his clothing. A six-pointed star was pinned to his buttonless vest, and his leather belt—over which his belly folded like fresh dough—was weighed down with a huge Walker Colt.

"And who are you?" Belle demanded, as the sheriff pulled to a halt in front of her. She was getting more exasperated by the minute, and this newcomer did not impress her at all.

"I am Sheriff Mike Emory, ma'am," he told her, his words slurring slightly. Then he looked foggily about him. "Now, what's this I hear about a holdup?" he asked.

The driver described the robbery, then added what Belle had just told him concerning Dean Stratemeyer. The sheriff, looking around at the faces pressing close upon him, cleared his throat nervously.

"Any of you men got horses so we can go after that feller? He maybe hurt hisself bad."

Not one hand went up, and not a single individual stepped forward.

"Hell, if he did hurt himself, that's his own durn fault," a man standing beside the sheriff asserted. As he did so, he glanced nervously at Belle.

"Forget it, Sheriff!" someone in back cried. "Ain't no one got a horse in this town. All we got is mules!"

There was a sharp bark of laughter at that. The sheriff looked at Belle. "Ma'am, these here are townsmen and miners. It's too late now to ride off after the Sonora Kid, and we ain't much for leaving Sonora just to look for a crazy man. An' he must've been crazy to jump off that stage like he did."

"Cowards and idiots!" snapped Belle. "Near as I can tell, there ain't a man here that's much of a hand at *anything*!"

She turned swiftly. With sudden, hushed respect, the townspeople parted before her as she steamed through their ranks toward the express office.

Sharon had witnessed the entire scene from the express office steps. She, too, had been concerned about the big, silent man who had thrown himself from the stage. Belle shook her head as she came to a halt beside Sharon. "What dolts!" She took a deep, indignant breath. "Well, I did what I could!"

"You certainly did," Sharon agreed. "And you have my admiration for it."

Sharon had already taken the liberty of having their trunks and other luggage sent on to the Sonora Hotel. It was an imposing, three-story brick edifice only a block down the street. Since it was reputed to be the finest hotel in Sonora, Belle was pleased and offered no objection as they set off for it.

"Where is that young gallant?" Belle asked Sharon. "The one who could not keep his eyes off you."

Sharon blushed. "He *was* very gallant, wasn't he?" she acknowledged. "He helped me with my bags, then hurried off. Poor man. He had been so confident before, so certain he would have no difficulty getting outfitted for the mines. But now he is practically penniless. It is all so sad."

"Don't worry about him," Belle counseled. "It was a terrible loss for him, but I'm sure he'll land on his feet. At least he had the gumption to stand up for a lady."

Sharon, recalling the incident, nodded her assent. "I hope you are right," she murmured. "About him landing on his feet, that is."

For her part, Belle was no longer so sure she had made the right move in coming to this rude outpost. She had not seen a man in that crowd she would have thrown a bone to if he were starving. A mealymouthed collection of unwashed half-wits—every blamed one of them.

It was all very depressing.

Rafe Barnett, in all the excitement, had slipped away through the crowd and proceeded to the Mexican quarter, where those Mexicans who had journeyed to Sonora to work the streams were now forced to live, along with the Californios.

The quarter was an untidy collection of shacks and log cabins—some with canvas for roofs—huddled in a steep-sided hollow, which drained rainwater and sewage from the rapidly expanding business district on the flats above them. In this mean, fog-enshrouded place, the mosquitoes were more numerous, the alleys more pungent, the streets narrower. Picking his way along them, Rafe came to a crude two-story hotel and checked in.

He settled into his room, tended to his toilet, changed his clothing, and sallied forth once again, heading back up the hill. Now he was dressed in immaculate, fawn-colored trousers, gleaming black leather boots, a silk shirt, and a string tie. His vest was of rich brocade, and he wore a high-crowned sombrero.

A few blocks past the new brick hotel was the Gold Nugget. Into this Barnett strode confidently. After finishing a beer at a table along the back wall, he got up and sauntered casually to the door at the far end of the bar. He knocked softly.

The door was pulled open, and Rafe was greeted by a tall, gaunt man in his early thirties with snow-white hair and a jet-black, handlebar mustache. Stepping aside to let Rafe in, the gaunt man closed the door swiftly; smiling broadly, he shook Rafe's hand warmly.

"You hear about it?" Rafe asked.

"I heard," replied Brett O'Hare. "Looks like José's taken another bite out of Finney's stage line."

A celebration of some sort was in order, it appeared. Taking out a thin cigar, O'Hare offered it to Rafe, after which he lit it for him with an expansive, mischievous flourish. His hand resting lightly on Rafe's back, O'Hare then led Rafe over to the flat-topped desk along the outside wall. O'Hare, smiling indulgently, watched as Rafe eased himself into the luxuriously cushioned swivel chair behind the desk.

"I saw the commotion when the stage pulled in," O'Hare said, sitting in another chair alongside the desk. "I watched what I could. Our sheriff is out in front at a table now, getting himself sloshed to celebrate the fact that he did not have to do anything. You want to tell me how it went?"

"That one who jumped from the stagecoach—he is the detective from Chicago. Of that I am certain. When José stopped the stage, I signaled him and he took the big fool's weapon first thing. Then José robbed him."

"What do you think? Will this guy give us any trouble?"

Rafe smiled coldly and shook his head. "He is a very brave man, I am sure—but he is also a fool. When he jumped from that stage, he had no weapon and no horse. If he overtakes José, José will kill him. If he does not overtake José—and the grizzlies do not get him—then I think he will arrive in Sonora one very tired detective."

O'Hare grinned. "How did José handle the rest?"

"Oh, there was some trouble. But he took my gold, as I told him, so there can be no suspicion of me."

"What kind of trouble?"

"He robbed the women passengers, and then he had to pistol-whip a passenger who did not like this. Perhaps he likes that hood too much. Maybe I should take it from him."

"You serious, Rafe? You want to get rid of José?"

Rafe considered a moment, then shook his head. "We will see. But I think for now we keep things as they are.

You will be the owner of the Gold Nugget, and I will be your friend. There is no need yet for these gringos to wonder why a Californio should have enough gold to own a saloon."

O'Hare nodded. "Any way you want it, Rafe."

"For now, that is the way I want it."

O'Hare got to his feet. "Guess I'll mosey back out there and keep that whiskey flowing down Sheriff Emory's gullet. Why not look over that ledger I been keeping for you? It's on the desk. Face it, Rafe, you're a wealthy businessman." O'Hare peered in a mirror and smoothed out his mustache. As he opened the door, he turned back and said, "There's more gold flowing across that mahogany bar out there than in all the damned streams in California."

For a short while, Rafe did as O'Hare had suggested, but then, restless, he pushed the faded blue ledger away from him and leaned back wearily in his chair. It had been a long, bone-jarring ride from Stockton, and he needed a breather.

This was the first time since purchasing the Gold Nugget that Rafe had walked into the saloon this openly. Serving as his front man, O'Hare had been running things nicely. It would not be long, however, before the citizens of Sonora would have to realize that their most popular saloon was owned outright by a Californio. When that time came, Rafe would welcome their consternation. Indeed, he would glory in it. But not now. He had many things yet to do before that day came.

Terrible things.

Rafe Barnett was in reality Rafael Escobar. In the two years since he had watched helplessly as his wife Josita placed the hangman's noose around her neck, the bitterness and sense of loss had grown within him, consuming him. Not a day went by that he did not think of his dead wife, nor a night when he did not lament her loss.

Two souls had died that night: Josita and the guitar-strumming, optimistic young man who had traveled north to the mines with her. To avenge her death, Rafael had become a murderer—an assassin—and whenever he allowed himself to think of what now remained of his immortal soul, he could only shudder.

It did not matter. He would let nothing—certainly not the threat of eternal damnation—prevent him from draining his cup of vengeance.

Already Rafe had seen to it that the hangman, the jury foreman, and two others had paid their debts in full. Of those Rafael had marked for extermination, only three remained alive: Colonel Hiram B. Polk, due soon in Sonora to participate in the Fourth of July celebrations; Jim Coleman, now a prosperous Sonora merchant; and Bill Finney, owner and operator of the Sonora Stage and Hauling Company.

Their string had just about run out. It was clear in his mind how he would deal with Colonel Polk. The forces that would destroy Bill Finney had already been set in motion. As to Jim Coleman, Rafael was only waiting for the opportune moment to finish him off—slowly—so that Coleman would know he was dying to avenge Josita Escobar's hanging.

Wearily, Rafe pulled the ledger closer to him once again. For the moment, he preferred to add and subtract numbers instead of souls.

Outside in the saloon, Brett O'Hare was at his usual table, presiding over a poker game. The game was winding down, with just him and a contentious miner still betting. The miner had matched O'Hare's last bet and now was calling him. With a shrug, O'Hare laid out two aces and three tens. *Full house*. Cursing violently, the miner threw down his three kings. He had been a sore loser throughout the last two games, and O'Hare took devilish pleasure in seeing through his transparent bluffs. Smirking, he reached out to gather in the pot.

"Damn your hide!" the miner cried, his bewhiskered face aflame with rage. "You palmed them two aces!" He jumped to his feet and glared down at O'Hare. The two other players hastily scraped their chairs back to get out of the line of fire. Still raking in his winnings, O'Hare glanced casually up at the miner.

"I suggest we go outside to settle this, Dilworth." There was a curious, almost grateful smile on O'Hare's face as he issued the invitation. "What do you say to that?"

"Suits me fine!" the miner snarled.

O'Hare got to his feet and carried the chips to the barkeep. He examined his revolver, then thrust it back into its holster and followed the miner out of the saloon. The patrons rushing through the swinging doors to watch the excitement almost trampled him. Their lust for the bloodshed soon to follow was so strong O'Hare could taste it. For these damned apes, he realized, there was nothing like a shooting to liven up an afternoon.

The miner was waiting in the middle of the street. At his side he held a huge Colt that appeared to be a Walker model, a heavy weapon. *I'll wager the fool don't know how to use it,* Brett thought. Then he left the porch and stepped out into the street.

At that moment Sheriff Emory stumbled out of the crowd toward him. Someone had obviously pushed him out as a joke.

"Now see here, Brett," the sheriff managed, staggering slightly. "Why don't you call this off? I don't want no trouble."

O'Hare pulled the sheriff's hat down over his face, spun him around, and shoved him roughly back into the crowd. Willing hands caught him and propelled him swiftly out of the way.

O'Hare eyed the miner, then cocked his Colt. The crowd went silent. Those in the front ranks cautiously pressed back. Ten or twelve paces away, the miner's enthusiasm for satisfaction seemed to be waning. He took a hesitant step forward. O'Hare, smiling serenely, stepped toward him as well. When the miner raised his oversized cannon, the heavy barrel wavered.

"You damn fool! Steady it!" O'Hare shouted at the man. "Use both hands!"

The miner took another step, the Walker still trembling

in his hand. O'Hare raised his own Colt and pulled up steadily, sighting along the barrel with quick precision at the miner's pale, grim face. He steadied the gun with his left hand and waited. Still the miner could not keep his weapon from wavering. O'Hare waited a moment longer, deliberately raised the barrel a notch, and sent a round over the miner's head.

Folding his arms calmly, O'Hare stuck the Colt back into his belt and waited for the miner to return his shot. Perspiring visibly now, the miner took still another step forward, steadied his aim as O'Hare had, and fired. The round exploded in the ground at O'Hare's feet.

"Try again, friend," urged O'Hare, arms still folded. His voice dripped with scorn. "Take another step closer. And this time, don't hurry your shot!"

"That's enough, Brett!" someone in the crowd shouted. "Don't be a fool!"

"Shoot the sonofabitch!" another cried.

Ignoring the comments, O'Hare smiled encouragingly at the miner—and waited.

Again the miner fired. This time the round snicked past O'Hare's right shoulder, taking a small piece of his frock coat with it.

"Much better," O'Hare told him. "We'll count that as a hit." Unfolding his arms then, he walked calmly past the miner on his way back into the saloon.

Rafe Barnett had come out of the saloon and was now standing on the saloon's porch, watching him. As O'Hare started up the steps to join him, he shouted, "Watch out, Brett!"

O'Hare spun just as the miner fired at him. The round from the Walker took a huge chunk out of the post beside O'Hare. Drawing his weapon almost reluctantly, O'Hare aimed swiftly and fired. The miner's right hand came apart in an explosion of blood and sinew, his weapon falling heavily to the ground. Howling in outrage and pain, the miner slipped to one knee, his face twisting in agony as he clasped his shattered hand.

Thrusting his revolver back into his belt, O'Hare

continued on into the saloon with Rafe, the excited, jubilant crowd swarming in after them. Once inside, O'Hare turned to face them. Doing his best to conceal the contempt he felt for each one of them, he shouted, "Drinks are on the house!"

As the barkeep hastened behind the bar to accommodate the rush, O'Hare turned to Rafe. "Take it out of my winnings." He shrugged as he turned away. "That poor sonofabitch of a miner was right, you know. Neither one of those aces came from the deck we were playing with."

Shaking his head, Rafe followed O'Hare into the office. Once they were inside, Rafe said, "Dammit, amigo! If I did not shout to you, you'd be one dead hombre! Do you *want* to die?"

O'Hare slumped down onto the leather couch against the wall. "Rafe, to run from death is to find him. Am I so important, anyway, that I should stomp out that insect's life to save my own?"

"You mean you feel pity for that miner?"

"Perhaps." O'Hare grinned. "He sure as hell was a lousy shot."

Rafe looked at O'Hare for a moment longer, then stared at the faded blue ledger as he remarked, "I will go back to these numbers now. I think they are not so complicated as you, amigo."

O'Hare swung his legs up onto the couch—to rest, not to sleep. He slept little, and this accounted in part for his wraithlike appearance. Closing his eyes now, he found himself once again recalling his dead wife. The trouble was that in his mind's eye, Ellen always appeared as she had looked the moment after he killed her.

For more than a year Ellen had been in excruciating pain from the cancer that ravaged her. And during all that time she had worked to convince him that he should spare her from this torment. He was her only hope. If he loved her, she insisted through her tears—*truly loved her*—he would not let her suffer any longer.

And since Brett O'Hare did love her—more than life

itself—he had at last acquiesced. Pinning her frail body beneath him, he held the pillow over her head, never expecting the writhing movements that soon became a strenuous effort to oppose him. When her fierce struggling ceased, he had lifted the pillow and gazed upon her.

Only a moment before she had been smiling up at him, encouraging him, blessing him for what he was about to do. Now her face was a mask of horror. A fearsome reproach. From that day to this, her distended tongue and protruding eyes—the terror of the unknown frozen on her face—had remained with him. Out of pity and compassion, he had killed the only woman he would ever love—and in her last moments, as she struggled futilely to throw him off, he was sure she was cursing him through all eternity for smothering the life out of her.

O'Hare moved restlessly on the couch. Had that miner not been such an abominable shot, he might now be crossing over to meet Ellen—either that or plunging into the sweet, blessed oblivion he craved.

Rafe glanced up from the ledger. "O'Hare . . ." he called softly. "Are you asleep?"

There was no response from O'Hare.

Rafe leaned back in his chair and gazed thoughtfully at his gringo friend. That this man could be asleep now convinced Rafe that for all O'Hare's talk of compassion, he felt nothing.

How else could one explain such supreme indifference in the face of death?

Chapter 3

Sharon had wasted no time. As soon as she had freshened up, she left the hotel and hurried to the Coleman Supply Emporium close to the edge of town. She could not miss it, the desk clerk had told her. And as she approached it, she realized what the clerk had meant.

Behind the store, on a fenced-in lot that must have covered at least five acres, she saw piles of freshly cut lumber and numberless bins containing wheelbarrows, picks, shovels, placer pans, and other goods and hardware needed by the army of miners swarming into this region. Bordering the near side of this lot were two huge storehouses, and from each of them came the unmistakable aroma of fresh grain and corn.

As she passed this sprawling cornucopia, Sharon shook her head. Clearly, this emporium was where most of the miners' wealth was going. Here was the real gold mine in Sonora.

She entered the store and proceeded down the nearest aisle until she came to the rear counter. A clerk was emptying a small keg of nails into a bin. He put the keg down hastily and ducked behind the counter to wait on her. His face had gone crimson at her appearance, and as he waited for her to arrive at the counter, he kept running his long fingers through his unruly shock of hair. He could not have been more than seventeen or eighteen.

"I'm looking for the owner, Mr. Jim Coleman, I believe," Sharon told him. "Is he about, please?"

"Oh, yes, ma'am," he said, nodding eagerly. "He's about."

"Would you be kind enough to fetch him for me?"

"Yes, ma'am. You wait right there!"

In his last letter to Sharon, Tim had mentioned that his partner in the diggings—Pete Wilder—had once worked for Jim Coleman, a store owner who ran supplies to their camp. She was now about to speak to this man, and her heart was pounding with excitement. She had come so far and was now so close to reaching Tim!

The clerk returned with Jim Coleman, then hurried back to work. Sharon disliked the store owner immediately. He appeared to her to be the kind of man who would just as soon sneak in through the back door as come in the front. A scrawny, balding man in his late forties, his shoulders were slightly stooped, the lines in his face all downcast. At first as he approached, he appeared almost apprehensive, almost frightened. But the moment his small, dark eyes caught sight of Sharon, an acquisitive gleam showed in them.

"I'm Jim Coleman, ma'am," the store owner said, pulling up on the other side of the counter. "You wanted to see me?"

"Mr. Coleman, I am Sharon Cortland. I have come all the way from Maine to find my brother. I think you can help me."

"I will if I can, ma'am." A slight, mocking light came into Coleman's eyes.

"Do you remember Pete Wilder? He used to work for you, I understand."

"I remember him."

"How long did he work for you?"

"A couple of weeks, maybe."

"You fired him?"

"He got gold fever. He only worked long enough to get a grub stake. Then he was off."

"Do you know where he is now, Mr. Coleman?"

"He's at the Pine Hill diggings."

Sharon could hardly believe her luck. This man not only remembered Tim's friend, he knew where to find him! "You mean he's there now?"

"Better be. He owes me considerable." He leaned forward then, his eyes gleaming. "If he's your brother, ma'am, I think you should know that he is in my debt. I would take it most kindly if you could see your way clear to wiping that considerable sum from my books."

"My brother is Tim Cortland. He is Mr. Wilder's partner, or was when he wrote me last. Perhaps you know my brother, as well."

"Tim Cortland, you say?"

"Yes." Sharon held her breath.

Coleman considered a moment, then shook his head. "Never heard of him."

Sharon sighed inwardly. For a moment there, she had been hoping for a miracle. But it was too much to expect that the first person she approached on arriving in Sonora would know the whereabouts of her brother. She comforted herself with the knowledge that in locating Tim's partner, she had taken a giant step toward finding Tim.

"I must get to this Pine Hill you mentioned so I may speak with Pete Wilder," Sharon told Coleman. "There's also the possibility, I am sure, that I will find Tim still in that mining camp with Mr. Wilder."

Coleman nodded. "Reckon that's a possibility, sure enough."

"Then perhaps you could tell me how to get there."

With sudden insolence, Coleman surveyed her from head to foot, his eyes crawling over her. Never had she felt so naked and unclean.

"Sure," Coleman said. "You can come along with me tomorrow morning. I got a shipment just about ready to leave for the Pine Hill diggings. I usually send it up with

one of my teamsters, but I'll go along myself on this trip so
you'll be safe." He smiled then in an effort to reassure
her. It had the opposite effect. "It'll take us a couple of
days. You think you'll be up to it?"

"I want to find my brother, Mr. Coleman," Sharon
replied stoutly.

"Be here, then. At sunup, no later."

"Yes. . . . Thank you, Mr. Coleman. You are very
kind."

The man nodded brusquely. "Just be on time."

He turned on his heels then, a somewhat different
man from the hesitant store owner who had greeted her a
moment before.

Though not at all sure she could trust Coleman, Sharon
was determined to go with him, nevertheless. She intended to reach the Pine Hill diggings, and she would do
so come hell or high water.

With this renewed determination, Sharon left the supply
store.

Hurrying back through the crowded streets toward
the hotel, she could not help noticing the incredible amount
of activity in this boomtown. It almost rivaled that of San
Francisco. *And what a city that is!* Sharon remembered as
she walked along.

When her ship had first entered San Francisco's harbor,
she had seen a forest of masts everywhere she looked.
Soon she had learned that they belonged to ships abandoned by their gold-hungry crews as soon as they docked.
Now these abandoned hulks filled most of the harbor.

Some of the larger boats, she marveled, were being
used as warehouses, while the port itself was being trans-
formed by the wagonloads of fill being dumped into the
coves to make more land. Above the city, hills were being
scraped raw, others flattened to provide still more fill.
Meanwhile, extensive wharfs were being constructed well
out into the waters past the derelict ships.

The only thing that mattered, Sharon soon found out,
was gold dust. Everywhere she went in San Francisco, she

found that prices were astronomical, the pace incredible. She saw men in full beards and expensive frock coats driving hacks, others on street corners peddling lots. Only a week before her ship docked, a terrible fire had raged through four city blocks, completely gutting them. Yet newer, taller buildings were springing up in the blackened ruins at a feverish pace. The city seemed to be rising like a phoenix from the ashes.

Before booking passage on a steamer upriver to Sacramento, she had been forced to take a room in a San Francisco hotel still under construction. The work had gone on throughout the night, with lanterns hanging from ropes and wires to give the workmen light, the sound of their rough conversation almost loud enough to drown out their incessant hammering and sawing. And as if that were not enough, as a background to this hive of activity, there had been the alarming clang of firebells and the angry, frantic barking of dogs as here and there about the city, isolated fires wiped out with careless abandon businesses or homes.

Under such conditions, of course, sleep had been impossible. Indeed, she realized suddenly, she hadn't had a good night's sleep since she left her ship in San Francisco. And from what she saw now as she walked down Sonora's Main Street, she knew sleep would not come easily in this bustling town either.

From all quarters she heard the rap of hammers and the steady buzz of handsaws. Hovels and ramshackle buildings—some of them built of unstripped logs and boasting only sagging canvas for roofs—were being torn down on almost every street, to be replaced with more substantial buildings. More than a few of these new buildings were of brick or fieldstone, and great freight wagons laden with such materials crowded the narrow streets. She saw men tearing down a structure while on the same site others were waiting to hastily build its successor.

Sharon shook her head dazedly. She was afraid the pace of California was getting to be too much for her.

Everything she had gazed upon since she reached here seemed to be in the process of becoming something else. Either that or it appeared to have arrived just yesterday or the day before. Sonora was only the last straw.

Sharon felt an utter weariness of spirit. She was more certain than ever that once she found her brother, she would waste no time in returning east with him to a more solid, less frantic world. Already she was aching for some sign of permanence, for cobblestoned streets and aged buildings begrimed with coal smoke—for the older, more stabilizing influences of civilized living. . . .

These fretful ruminations were rudely ended when a crowd of men rushed toward Sharon and swept past her, breaking from the sidewalk and charging across the street in the direction of a saloon less than a block behind her. In their heedless rush they almost ran over her, and it had taken some doing for Sharon to keep moving against their swarming tide.

Glancing back in some alarm, she saw a crowd forming around two men facing each other in the middle of the street. One appeared to be a miner, the other a white-haired cadaverous fellow dressed in a frock coat.

And each one held a revolver in his hand!

Horrified, Sharon hurried on, reached the hotel, and ducked inside. At that moment she heard shots being fired. Those few guests remaining in the lobby rushed from it at once, leaving an unsettled Sharon standing alone in the middle of the room. She had an irrational impulse to run somewhere and hide, but she knew that such a response would be lacking in courage. It might be she had migrated to the site of an insane asylum—she was growing more positive she had—but that did not mean she should act without courage or fortitude.

Even as she thought this, she spied Belle Harper standing before the doorway to the hotel's dining room. She looked positively handsome in a bottle-green dress that followed her robust figure closely all the way past her hips, where it flared saucily at the ankles in an explosion of lace. Even from where Sharon was standing, she could

see how recklessly Belle's neckline plunged, framing the
twin strands of pearls that gleamed on her bosom.

Belle caught sight of her at the same time and with a
quick motion of her hand invited Sharon to join her.
Pleased and grateful for the invitation, Sharon hurried
over to her friend.

"Where have you been?" Belle asked, when Sharon
reached her. "I rapped on your door as soon as I got
settled in. You sure didn't waste any time lightin' out. You
got friends in town?"

"Let's go in and sit down," Sharon said with a weary
smile. "I'll tell you all about it."

Looking at Sharon with sudden concern, Belle nodded.
"Do that, child. You look to me like you just finished
wrestling with the devil himself. You're as pale as them
tablecloths in there. Follow me. I'll find us a nice quiet
corner."

Belle was as good as her word. She led Sharon to a
small table in a corner, and after they had ordered, she
leaned close and smiled encouragingly.

"Out with it, now. Where were you?"

Sharon told her of her visit to Jim Coleman's emporium and of his promise to take her with him to the Pine
Hill diggings, where there was a good chance she might
pick up her brother's trail. She also told Belle about
Coleman's manner and what it undoubtedly implied. Finishing up, she shook her head in some discouragement
and admitted to Belle how weary she had suddenly become of California.

"Letdown," Belle said. "Feel it myself. Only natural,
dearie. We've had a long, wretched voyage, and now that
we're here, we find it is even worse than the places we
left—a whole lot worse. Where we come from, the men
took baths on Saturdays, at least."

Sharon laughed nervously. The waitress brought them
the wine Belle had insisted on ordering as an aperitif.
Sharon lifted her glass somewhat uncertainly, but Belle
did not hesitate. With a broad wink, she downed half the
glass. Sharon followed suit. She did not drink often, but as

the wine kindled a path down her throat and into her bosom, she almost instantly felt much better. On an impulse, she drained the glass.

"Easy does it, dearie," Belle said with a smile. "Don't want to overdo a good thing."

"I'd like another glass," Sharon exclaimed. "I feel better already."

Belle laughed and finished her own drink as well. "A whole lot looser, anyway, I'll bet." She waved their waitress over and ordered more wine. Then she looked sternly across at Sharon and said, "I'm curious. I am sure your instincts about this fellow Coleman are sound. So what are you going to do about him?"

"Keep an eye on him."

"My dear, what assurance do you have that keeping an eye on him will make you any safer?"

"I have to take the chance, Belle. How else can I get to Pine Hill? Don't worry. If he tries anything unpleasant, I'll make things very unpleasant for *him*."

Belle sighed. "I suppose you don't have much choice. Good luck, dearie."

Just then a host of miners and a few hotel patrons began streaming into the dining room. In loud, excited voices, which they made no effort to lower, they recounted the spectacular shootout they had just witnessed in front of the Gold Nugget. Only gradually did the uproar subside.

About then the two women's supper arrived, and as they ate, Sharon confided in Belle her sense of the exasperating impermanence of all she had encountered. Belle understood what Sharon was feeling. She, too, was longing for the stability she had left behind on this reckless search for a rich husband.

"Sometimes I think I must have gone crazy," Belle admitted. "Along with every other gold-maddened fool who set out for this place. But I'm here now. And so are you. So we might as well make the best of it." She smiled cheerfully then. "What say we finish up with another glass of wine. I think we deserve it."

They drank their third glass slowly, savoring the wine's fruity bouquet, unwilling to see this pleasant meal come to an end. When the waitress brought their check, Belle generously insisted on paying it. Giving up her protest at last, Sharon promised to return the favor when she arrived back from the diggings with her brother.

As they walked from the dining room, Sharon felt slightly giddy. She realized she had perhaps imbibed a little too heartily, but only momentarily was she perturbed at this state of affairs. After all, she told herself, it was about time she felt good about something.

The two of them were walking very close so as not to weave too noticeably, when a large, handsome man in his late forties planted himself in front of them. He was powerfully built, with immense shoulders and girth. Big though he was, there was apparently not an ounce of surplus tallow on his frame. Ruddy of complexion, he had dark, laughing eyes and coal-black, curly hair. Whipping off his hat, he bowed with elaborate politeness.

"Ma'am," he said, looking Belle boldly in the eyes, "I have been searching high and low for you!"

"For me?" Belle replied, surprised.

"Yes. Allow me to introduce myself. I am Ted Manders. I saw you this afternoon when you lit into that fool sheriff and the rest of those craven misfits. I was watching from my hotel window, you see, or I would have been at your side, adding my voice to yours. As it is, all I can do now is tell you how much I admired your fire."

"That so?" Belle was obviously pleased.

"Indeed, it is." He paused, a look of comic unhappiness passing over his heavily lined face. "But I see my luck is bad once again. I am too late to escort you to supper. Perhaps you will allow me to join you tomorrow morning for breakfast."

"Mister," Belle observed, "you don't even know my name."

He smiled. "Indeed, you have the advantage on me, I am afraid."

Belle was unable to resist his sincere smile. She gave him her name, then introduced Sharon. Manders took Sharon's hand gallantly in his and brushed it with a kiss. He was a rough and ready fellow who at the moment seemed to be enjoying himself hugely.

Turning back to Belle, Manders's dark eyes locked with hers. "Breakfast then, Belle. And what would be a good time for you?"

Belle smiled saucily. "Give me some time to pull myself together. How would eight-thirty be?"

"Fine. The lobby at eight-thirty, Belle. Until then."

Clapping his hat back on, he touched its brim to both of them and swept on past them. Joining a male companion who had been waiting for him at the door, he disappeared into the dining room.

Belle looked after the big man for a moment, then turned to Sharon, her eyes alight. "Now that," she said, "is a man very difficult to say no to. I'd better watch myself."

"Not too closely, Belle," Sharon retorted, laughing gaily—perhaps just a little too gaily.

"Dearie," Belle said, "I think you're feeling a mite silly."

Sharon nodded happily. Then she clasped her hand quickly over her mouth to prevent a giggle.

Doing her best to keep a straight face, Belle said, "I think I had better see you to your room."

"Yes," Sharon agreed. "I think you better."

José Morales kept himself erect by leaning against the rear door of the Gold Nugget. He was out of breath and panting heavily. After a while he managed to slam his fist against the door. But there was no response. Glancing feverishly up and down the dark alley, he swore bitterly in Spanish, drew his six-gun, and clubbed the door with it. He did this twice, viciously.

Someone pulled the door open. It was the saloon's swamper. José slumped forward across the threshold and promptly lost consciousness. The swamper, an emaciated, rake-handle of a man who drank too much, gave up trying to drag José all the way into the hallway and went off to fetch help.

The swamper appeared a moment later with O'Hare, who at first seemed stunned by what he saw. Then he bent quickly and dragged José into the hallway as the swamper slammed the door shut and then threw the bolt.

"Give me a hand, Slim," O'Hare told the swamper. "We'll take him into my office. Then I want you to forget all about this."

"Sure thing, boss."

The two men lugged José down the dim hallway and into the office. As soon as they reached the doorway, a startled Rafe hurried to assist them. After dropping José onto the couch, O'Hare looked quickly up and down the hallway, then closed the door.

O'Hare made a quick examination of the unconscious man. José was breathing irregularly, and his pale face glistened with perspiration. O'Hare had seen the bullet hole in José's back when he was sprawled over the threshold. Reaching in under him now, O'Hare felt for the wound. The hole was just under José's right shoulder blade. O'Hare glanced up at Slim, who was about to leave the office.

"Hold on, Slim," he said. "Is Doc Wraither out there?"

"Last I saw, he was. At a table in the back."

"Get him."

Slim nodded and vanished out the door.

O'Hare stood up and looked unhappily at Rafe. "Looks like that crazy operative from Chicago—the one who jumped out of the stage—wasn't so crazy, after all."

Swearing softly, Rafe nodded his head in assent. "How bad is José?"

"Bad enough. He's got a hole as big as my thumb in his back. And he's lost a lot of blood from the look of him."

"There was no horse outside?"

"No horse. And no gold."

Again Rafe swore.

O'Hare bent over José a second time and went through his pockets. From José's tight-fitting trousers, he took the black silk hood and handed it to Rafe, who saw that it was bloodstained. At one point, José must have tried to stop the bleeding with it. Swiftly Rafe retreated to the file cabinet behind his desk. Pulling open a drawer, he dropped the hood into it.

He stayed behind the desk. "Anything else?"

Straightening up, O'Hare threw a small emerald brooch at him and then a set of earrings.

Rafe did not have to examine them to know to whom they had belonged. "Is that all?"

"That's all."

Rafe dumped the jewelry onto the hood and slammed the file shut. Then he slumped into his chair. It wasn't so much José Morales that concerned him now. He was thinking of the operative, Dean Stratemeyer. A big, slow-moving man, he had thought. Too slow, maybe, to get out of his own way. Nothing to worry about. When he had plunged from the stage, Rafael had considered him a fool given to making futile gestures.

But no longer.

A little after nine that night, an exhausted Dean Stratemeyer rode into Sonora. He was riding a bay gelding with two fat saddlebags draped over the pommel. Though it was completely dark at the time, anyone who took the time to look closely would have seen a dark smear of dried blood on the bay's flanks. But no one looked closely. No one paid much attention at all as the weary Stratemeyer rode through the narrow, crowded streets, looking for the office of Bill Finney's Sonora Stage and Hauling Company.

The last couple of miles into Sonora had been considerably easier than the preceding six on foot. The Sonora Kid's bloody spoor had not been difficult to follow, and when Stratemeyer had come upon the Kid's abandoned mount just before sundown, he knew how much blood the outlaw had lost and was disappointed not to find a body—dead or unconscious—somewhere close by.

Reaching Finney's express office, Stratemeyer dismounted. A young clerk was behind the counter working over a huge ledger. He looked up as Stratemeyer entered, and put down his pen hastily.

"We're closed, sir," the clerk told the bearlike man.

"No, you're not. I just walked in. You know the combination to the safe?"

Apprehensively, the clerk nodded. The thought was evidently occurring to him that Stratemeyer was about to rob the company.

"Good," replied Stratemeyer. "Come outside with me. I've got some gold that belongs to your boss. I want you to put it in the safe overnight."

Relieved, the clerk followed Stratemeyer out to his horse. It took both of them to lug the heavy leather saddlebags into the office. Afterward, Stratemeyer slumped into a chair and suggested the clerk take the gold from the leather sacks and place it in the safe. The clerk did as he was told, stacking the gleaming coins in neat, shiny rows. Stratemeyer watched closely, making sure the young man didn't disturb the other valuables in the bags.

Finished at last, the clerk swung the huge safe door shut.

Stratemeyer pushed himself wearily to his feet. "Tell your boss I'll be in to see him first thing in the morning."

The amazed clerk simply nodded.

Taking the saddlebags and mounting up again, Stratemeyer rode back to a livery he had passed earlier, dismounted, and led the horse inside. An old, stove-up cowboy put aside his pitchfork and took the bay's reins.

"Two bits," the hostler told him. "Four bits if you want oats."

"That's right. Oats and water and rub him down some." Stratemeyer tossed the hostler four bits and a little extra.

Lifting the now lightweight saddlebags off the bay, Stratemeyer left the stable and walked across the street to the Sonora Hotel. There was a great deal of money inside the bags that should be returned to its rightful owners, Stratemeyer knew. But he was too far gone now to search out the two men. He would find them tomorrow, he promised himself wearily as he signed the hotel register and mounted the steps to his room.

He managed to kick off his boots before sprawling face down onto the bed, and before the mattress finished rocking under him, he was asleep.

Chapter 4

J im Coleman had told Sharon to be at his store at sunup.
She arrived before dawn. Packing all she would need for
her journey into one of her two large carpetbags, she had
lugged it all the way from the hotel through the damp,
predawn darkness. Many men had passed by her, but not
a single one had offered her help.

No light came from the store. Concluding that no one
had yet shown up for the day's business, including Jim
Coleman, she picked up the carpetbag and carried it around
to the back of the building. The gate leading into the
warehouse compound was open, and when she entered,
she saw in the dim light enormous freight wagons lined up
like patient beasts. From a large converted Conestoga
wagon at the head of the line came the dim mutter of
voices. She headed for it.

When she stopped beside the wagon, a vaguely familiar figure was clambering down from the top of the load.
Dropping to the ground, the man turned to face her. It
was Dan Prentiss.

"Why, Miss Cortland!" Dan cried, startled. "What
are you doing here at this hour?"

"I could ask you the same question." She was sur-

43

prised at the wave of relief that she felt upon seeing him.

"I work here," Dan told her. "I got the job last night. By the time that Sonora Kid finished with me, I had less than ten dollars left. Working here is a far cry from digging for gold, but it will have to do for now."

Sharon was impressed. Such ill fortune would have been enough to finish most men, but Dan Prentiss seemed to have recovered nicely. As Belle had already remarked, he was the type to land on his feet. It would take more than financial loss to stop Dan Prentiss.

There was enough light now for Sharon to see the mark where the Sonora Kid had struck him. The cruel blow had left an ugly, purplish welt.

Frowning in sudden concern, Sharon asked, "How does your face feel? That was a terrible blow you took."

He shrugged. "Nothing to worry about. I'm sorry about you losing that brooch."

"I shouldn't have carried on so," she told him.

"It must have been of great importance to you."

"It was a present from my brother. He gave it to me the year he left for California."

"I remember now. You mentioned you had come out here to find him. He is very lucky to have a sister as devoted as you. I hope you find him."

She smiled. "That's what I am doing here now. There's a good chance Tim is at the Pine Hill diggings. Mr. Coleman has consented to take me there."

Dan's warm expression changed abruptly. "You mean you're going all the way to the Pine Hill diggings with Jim Coleman? Alone?"

"Why, yes, I am," she replied. "But there's no need to make it sound so ominous. I am sure I will be perfectly safe with Mr. Coleman—"

"I wish I were as sure as you are."

"Really, Mr. Prentiss. I think you will have to let me be the judge of who is or who is not a threat to me."

Immediately chagrined, he said, "Call me Dan. Please.

And I am sorry if I presumed too much. You have my apologies."

"Apologies?" asked Jim Coleman, emerging from the shadows. He was coming from the direction of the store. "Have you been bothering Miss Cortland, Prentiss?"

"Of course he hasn't," Sharon spoke up. "Dan and I are old friends. He was not bothering me at all."

Coleman nodded curtly. "Very well."

Turning to Dan, Coleman asked if he had finished loading the wagon. When Dan told him he had, Coleman, a bill of lading in his hand, made a swift inspection of the load. Satisfied, he told Dan to fetch the horses. As Dan hurried off, Coleman looked at Sharon and smiled—as pleasantly as he was able.

"Guess you do know how to get to a place on time, at that," he said. "As soon as Prentiss gets those horses hitched, we'll move out." He noticed the carpetbag on the ground beside Sharon. "That your bag?"

Sharon nodded.

Coleman bent and heaved it up onto the wagon behind the seat. He was not at all careful, and Sharon winced as it lodged heavily between two barrels.

"You'll ride up front with me," Coleman told her as Dan appeared with the horses. "Maybe you can help me drive the team some."

"Of course, Mr. Coleman. I'll be glad to help all I can."

He smiled again. It was just as unpleasant the second time. Sharon thought it was probably because when Coleman smiled, the smile never reached his eyes.

"You can call me Jim," he remarked. "And I'll just call you Sharon."

Sharon did not reply. Instead, she hugged herself slightly to keep off the chill, the one brought by the damp wind of early morning—and by the cold, calculating gleam in Coleman's eyes.

Dan Prentiss watched grimly as Jim Coleman pulled out of the yard, Sharon Cortland sitting up beside him on the wagon seat. Dan had waved to Sharon and she had waved back. Hers had been a tentative, uncertain wave, however, and Dan got the distinct impression that she was not nearly as sure of herself and of her situation as she wanted him to believe.

He stood by the gate until the wagon disappeared, then headed for the store, untying his heavy apron as he walked. Inside, he found the store manager dragging a sack of chicken feed over toward an empty bin. The manager glanced up as Dan approached, and he appeared relieved to see him.

"I could use a hand here, Prentiss," he said, straightening up. "Where you been?"

"Helping Coleman load up that wagon for Pine Hill."

"You can finish this, then. I have to get back to the office."

"Sorry," Dan said, handing his neatly folded apron to the manager.

"Now what in tarnation is this supposed to mean?" the manager asked, taking the apron from Dan.

"I'm quitting."

"Now? But last night you pleaded for this job!"

"That was last night. Also, I'm borrowing one of your boss's saddle horses. And some supplies. I'll bring the horse back in fine shape—and the price of the supplies in gold dust."

"You can't do that!"

"Sure I can. Watch me."

He left the manager and strode through the store and out the rear door, heading toward one of the stables. There was no way he was going to let Jim Coleman spend a night alone with Sharon Cortland. Dan had overheard one of the clerks the night before remarking at this sudden decision of Coleman's to take the supplies himself to the Pine Hill diggings. Why Coleman was willing to spend two days on the trail when he usually sent one of his teamsters had the clerk wondering.

But Dan did not need to wonder. He knew why.

*   *   *

When Belle Harper had appeared at the dining room entrance that morning for breakfast, Ted Manders had beamed. Wearing a dress entirely of white, Belle seemed almost angelic to Ted, and he rushed to escort her to their table.

Now, their breakfast finished, Ted Manders was not content to part with Belle. After admitting to her that the source of his wealth was a gold mine in the hills less than five miles from Sonora, he prevailed upon her to ride with him out to the mine itself. After the mildest demurral Belle consented, but she insisted that he give her time for changing into dress more suitable for such an expedition.

When she left the hotel with Manders less than an hour later, a small crowd gathered to watch their departure. Manders had driven up to the hotel in a gleaming surrey, drawn by two spirited blacks. Belle now wore a navy blue dress, incredibly small at the waist and with a cloud of white lace at her throat. She was carrying a parasol of the same material, and an insubstantial shawl rested on her shoulders. The wide brim of her white hat was bent stylishly over her face. Peering almost mischievously out from under the brim, Belle's blue eyes seemed to have gained intensity and beauty as she smiled at Manders and allowed him to assist her into the surrey.

As Manders climbed in beside her and took up the reins, an impulsive cheer went up from the small crowd of onlookers. Smiling rakishly at Belle, Manders snapped the whip and set the horses to a sprightly trot, which he kept up until they were well out of town.

Manders had already told Belle what he did before coming to California. One of three partners in a thriving concern selling building supplies in Philadelphia, he had sold his interest and booked passage on a packet that took him to California via Cape Horn. Like Belle, he had not enjoyed the voyage, and each was able to regale the other with stories that now—only after the ordeal was over—were able to rouse them to laughter. Belle told of one man so sick that as they rounded the Cape, he leaned over the rail and lost both his uppers and lowers.

At last, exhausted from laughter, Belle asked Manders about this mine he was so anxious to show her. Was it like a coal mine, she wanted to know, a shaft sunk into the ground, from which tunnels radiated out into the earth?

"Nothing like that, Belle," Manders told her. "At least not for now. Though we may come to that."

"Then how do you mine the gold?"

"At first it was sufficient simply to pan for it. You do know about panning, don't you?"

"Well, I've heard a little about it. But I'd like to know more."

"I'm delighted to oblige," he replied, smiling broadly. "But allow me to start from the beginning. As near as I can figure, there is a mother lode somewhere above us in the mountains. From this lode, gold is being leached by the water seeping through the ground. As this water finds its way into the streams draining the region, it deposits tiny particles of gold in the streams. So what we have been doing is removing the gold from the mud and silt in the streams and rivers. And from the banks above them, as well."

"And how do you do that?"

"We place the silt or mud from the streams in a pan. Then, with a gentle, rotating motion, we slosh away the dirt over the sides of the pan until only the gold remains. Since the gold is heavier than the dirt and other particles, it sinks to the bottom of the pan. Then it is removed and the process is repeated with more samples of mud and silt."

"Sounds tedious."

"It is that. Backbreaking, as well. Still, with this method, I have seen miners remove as much as fifty thousand dollars in gold from a stream—and that in only one day's work. At one such digging, a single pan could yield as much as two thousand dollars or more at a time."

"Where was this?" Belle asked in some astonishment.

"Rich Bar."

Belle laughed and shook her head. "That's certainly an appropriate name. Is it near here?"

"No, and it has been pretty well cleaned out by now, anyway."

"Then it is true. Great wealth awaits those who come here."

Manders frowned thoughtfully before responding. "Great wealth and great tragedy, I'm afraid, Belle. Not every man who has come seeking gold in these hills has been able to survive the backbreaking labor of digging for it. Many of the greenhorns have already left, discouraged. Others have died here with the cholera, or worse than that, from rum. When I recall what happened to one of my shipboard companions . . . well, it makes you wonder."

"Tell me about him," Belle said.

"His name was John Foley. Back east he was a successful lawyer and a member of the Maine legislature. Soon after we arrived in San Francisco, I lost track of him. But one night, in a camp north of here, I was resting in a rented bunk when I heard a fearful clamor, and into the camp roared this drunken lunatic. At first I didn't recognize him; then I realized it was my old shipboard friend, John.

"But there was no way I could get him to recognize me and settle down. He was yelling and screaming as if a legion of fiends were after him. He was barefooted, bareheaded, and barelegged. He had nothing on except a shirt, and I soon learned he had been roaming about the camp for close to a week in that pitiable condition. Not long after, screaming like a screech owl, he bolted from the camp and disappeared into the wilderness. I never heard of him again."

Belle shuddered. "But what could have caused such a change?"

"Drink and despair. Having no luck, he abandoned himself to the bottle and ended up nothing more than a raving maniac, a poor, miserable, crazy vagabond. And I've seen it happen to others. I've also seen a Yale professor give up on the mines and turn to freight handling."

"A Yale professor?" Belle was astonished.

Manders laughed and nodded. "We've got plenty of

lawyers here, too. But damn few of them have found gold—except one fellow who became a mule-team driver for one hundred twenty-five dollars a month. He'll get his gold the slow way."

Belle shook her head, then peered with renewed interest at Manders. "And how, Ted Manders, do you get your gold?"

He laughed. "We have only a mile to go now," he told her. "You'll soon see."

What Belle saw when she got there was a vast drained stream bed being gouged by great toothed buckets. On the ends of long lines of cable were buckets spewing out huge mouthfuls of dirt onto the banks of the riverbed. Attacking these mounds of dirt were men with wheelbarrows. They were busy transporting portions of the dirt over narrow catwalks to drums, which were now furiously whirling. The drums themselves were constructed rather crudely of chicken wire, it appeared to Belle, and the roar from them was constant. What their purpose was, Belle had not the slightest idea.

"But where's the river?" Belle asked, as Manders reached up and helped her down from her seat.

"Diverted," Manders said, pointing to a log-sided flume in the woods off to the right. "My partners and I spent one entire winter building a dam and that flume to divert the water. Once we channeled the water into a ravine nearby, we had a riverbed to exploit. It was a gamble, but we were lucky. We've taken quite a bit of gold from this bed."

"And your partners? Where are they?"

"I bought them out. They wanted to find richer diggings."

"And did they?"

"Yes. In Amador County. They believe they have found the mother lode. And if you think this operation here is something, you ought to inspect theirs. They are actually attacking the mountainsides with water, washing out the gold in that fashion. I suppose you could call it hydraulic mining. Already they have blasted out a gulch that's a mile long."

Belle glanced past Manders to watch the men pushing their wheelbarrows over the narrow, jouncing catwalks. Moving closer to the edge of the riverbank, she saw still other miners toiling far below her. They were digging at the banks with picks and shovels, while still deeper in the bowels of the riverbed, she glimpsed machines clawing at the earth with gleaming, iron teeth. And all of this she was forced to view through a whirling, humming network of water-driven belts and pulleys.

Momentarily dizzy, she stepped back.

Manders moved quickly up beside her. "Are you all right?" he asked, obviously concerned.

"I'm fine," she told him. "There's just so much to see." Then she pointed to the rapidly whirling drums she had noticed earlier. The miners on the catwalks were dumping load after load of dirt into them. "Why are the men dumping the dirt into those wire drums?" she asked.

"Those drums are trommels. They sift the sand and gravel being dumped into them."

She shaded her eyes. "I can see something sifting down from each of the drums. Is that the gold?"

"Close to it. As the dirt washes over those ribs in the flumes below the trommels, the gold dust lodges against them."

Belle nodded. What had appeared incomprehensible a moment before was clear enough now. Everything she saw was simply a method for getting enormous amounts of dirt from the riverbed to those drums, where it could be sifted—after which its precious gold could be removed. There was certainly no romance in all this grubbing for gold—only grimy little men laboring like ants in an anthill.

Belle turned and started back to the surrey. She felt a little foolish all of a sudden in her lace-trimmed dress and matching parasol. Manders helped her back up into the seat.

"I must leave you for a minute," he told her. "I have

some business with my foreman. Will you be all right here?"

"Of course," she said, smiling. "Find out how much gold you have left."

Manders winced. "Don't remind me. We've already taken quite a bit out of this dig." With a quick bow, he started along a narrow path that led off the embankment and down into the ravaged stream bed.

He returned less than a quarter of an hour later. As he approached, he managed a smile for her, but it was not an easy one. She looked closely at him as he climbed up beside her and gathered in the reins.

"Is something wrong, Ted?"

"Wrong? What could possibly be wrong on a day that has begun this famously? I suggest a leisurely drive back to Sonora, and then dinner."

"You're very kind."

He reached over and squeezed her hand gently. "It is you, Belle, who are kind—to bless this hopelessly masculine life of mine with your great beauty and warmth. There is no gold in all this earth that shines as brightly as a woman's smile."

Belle blushed and said nothing. Ted Manders was a gallant, extravagant man. So gallant was he that he had obviously chosen not to tell her whatever disturbing news he had learned from his foreman, and so extravagant was he in his praise that he warmed the cockles of her heart. She would find it surprisingly easy not only to respect this man, but also to love him.

An alarm bell rang deep inside her. *Hold on!* she told herself. *Isn't it a little too soon for you to start thinking like this? You met this gentleman only last night!*

The crack of the whip broke into her thoughts as Manders started up, and soon they were plunging back through the forest the way they had come—the intoxicating, pine-scented wind blowing in her face erasing all thought of caution.

Dean Stratemeyer had emerged from the hotel just as

Belle and Manders were driving off earlier that morning. He was sorry to have missed her. Had he had a chance to speak to Belle, he might have been able to learn the whereabouts of the other two male passengers. He was still packing their money and was anxious to return it to them.

The surrey drove off. Stratemeyer crossed the street, breakfasted in a small restaurant, then set off for the Sonora Stage and Hauling Company's express office.

Standing on the front platform of the office in the midst of a small, excited crowd was the clerk who had helped him stash the recovered gold the night before. The instant the clerk saw Stratemeyer approaching, he abruptly left the crowd and bolted into the express office. Almost at once a man Stratemeyer assumed was Bill Finney charged from the office and hurried down the boardwalk toward him, the crowd rushing after.

"You must be Stratemeyer," Bill Finney cried when he reached Stratemeyer, pumping his hand excitedly. "You have no idea how pleased I am to meet you! And to thank you!"

"And you must be Bill Finney," observed Stratemeyer, "the owner of the stage line."

"Of course. My clerk just told me! You brought in the gold last night! All of it!" Finney continued to shake Stratemeyer's hand.

The crowd had closed about them by this time and was hanging on every word the two spoke. Mildly annoyed, Stratemeyer brushed past Finney and continued on toward the office.

"I'd rather not discuss this out here," he told the owner.

With a quick, anxious nod, Finney followed the detective through the crowd and into the express office. The clerk, as excited as his boss, followed after them, but Finney instructed the young man to go back outside and see that no one disturbed them. Then he led Stratemeyer into his inner office.

"Good news has a way of spreading," Finney explained happily, slumping into the chair behind his desk. "I am sure you can understand how pleased everyone is."

Stratemeyer sat in a straight-backed chair by the desk and took out a cigar. Lighting it, he said, "I don't suppose you thought of telling that clerk of yours to keep his mouth shut."

"I did," Finney said lamely, "but I was too late. Besides, Mr. Stratemeyer, such news is too good to keep a secret for long. I can now pay my workers and meet my loan at the bank. Those new stagecoaches of mine were shipped around the Cape all the way from Portland and cost a pretty penny, I can assure you. The bank was about to foreclose. You've saved my shirt, Mr. Stratemeyer."

"For the moment, perhaps."

"Why do you say that?"

"I still don't have the Sonora Kid."

"What?" Finney blurted, frowning suddenly. "What did you just say?"

Stratemeyer drew calmly on his cigar, then exhaled. "You heard what I said, Finney. I don't have the Kid."

Finney was flabbergasted. "Why, man, what are you saying? The gold in that safe over there was stolen by the Sonora Kid—and you brought it back. Surely, you must have apprehended him! My God, Mr. Stratemeyer, that's what my clerk has been telling everyone."

"I am not responsible for what that fool clerk of yours says. When I brought that gold in here, I told him nothing. I did not apprehend the Sonora Kid. I wounded him—that much is true. But he got clean away and managed to slip into Sonora before I could overtake him."

Finney slumped wearily back into his chair, his elation of a moment before vanishing instantly. The transformation in his appearance was remarkable. The man looked years older. He was in his late thirties and would have passed for a handsome man if he had not become so gaunt. His mustache was well kept and he combed his sleek, black hair straight back. But the slack gave to his shoulders and the deep, haunting melancholy in his eyes gave the impression of a man holding himself together with baling twine.

Staring bleakly at Stratemeyer, Finney muttered, "I knew all along it was too good to be true." He sighed and shook his head. "A year ago I was ready to bring a wife from New York. Then the Kid began this string of robberies. Lately, I've been having trouble everywhere. I had a fire two weeks ago. Lost a warehouse. I tell you, Stratemeyer, I am in trouble. Deep trouble."

"I sympathize, Finney. Believe that. See if you can't hang on a mite longer. I've seen the Kid without his hood, so I know what he looks like. He's a dark, raw-boned young man of Mexican extraction. Sonora has a Mexican quarter, I understand. Has any word about the Sonora Kid come from that part of town? There is a good chance, is there not, that he has perhaps become somewhat of a hero to his fellow Mexicans?"

"If he's a Mex, that's likely, I'll admit. I haven't heard anything, though. But then I never go near that quarter, and none of my friends do."

Stratemeyer shrugged and got to his feet. "All right. I'll get back to you as soon as I have anything more."

"You do that," Finney said wearily. "But there is one thing you should know. I hired two men, both of them from San Francisco. Tough men, they were. Veritable bloodhounds. They took after the Sonora Kid—and disappeared. I have no doubt at all what happened to them. They've been dropped in a gulley somewhere in the hills above Sonora—a bullet in each of their backs."

Stratemeyer smiled. "Are you trying to warn me or encourage me?"

"Neither. I just thought you ought to know."

"Thanks, but Pinkerton already told me about my two predecessors."

"And you took this assignment anyway?"

Stratemeyer pulled his gray fedora down more securely. "Hell, yes. This job wouldn't be any fun at all if it didn't have risk attached." With that he turned and strode from the office.

Some members of the crowd were still hanging around in front of the express office, and Stratemeyer discouraged them by brushing brutally through without a single backward glance. Once he had shaken them, he headed for the livery stable where he had left the Kid's horse.

He found the bay in a rear stall. The old hostler had brushed down and curried the gelding with such enthusiasm that his coat was gleaming, all trace of the bloodstain gone. With a lantern he took down from a nail, Stratemeyer examined the bay's flanks carefully. He had hoped to see a brand, but he was not too surprised when he found none. The Sonora Kid would not be dumb enough to ride a horse that could be easily traced.

Stratemeyer sought out the hostler and found him busy currying a powerful chestnut. The two men introduced themselves. The hostler's name was Jake Gater. After complimenting the old cowpoke on the excellent care he had given the bay, Stratemeyer asked Gater if he had ever seen the gelding in his livery stable before last night.

"Nope," Gater said. "Can't say as I have. Nice piece of horseflesh. Where'd you get him?"

"Picked him up about a couple of miles outside town."

Gater peered at Stratemeyer shrewdly. "You're the detective who brought in the gold, ain't you. I been hearing about you."

"I'm the one."

"There was blood on that bay. Dried blood. It wasn't yours, so I reckon it must've been the Sonora Kid's."

"That's a good enough guess."

"And you was hoping the Kid might be stupid enough to rob a stage on a horse he rented from the stable. If he was that stupid, mister, I would know who he was."

Stratemeyer grinned. "Pretty farfetched, I admit. Didn't think it would do any harm to ask."

"Oh it didn't!" Gater let fly a dart of black tobacco juice from the corner of his mouth. "But like I said, I ain't never saw that mount in here before last night. Last time I clapped eyes on that bay, it was tied up at the hitchrack in front of the Gold Nugget."

With a sudden grin, Stratemeyer thanked the hostler and left the stable.

The Gold Nugget was nearly empty this early in the morning. Halfway down the bar, a bedraggled sot was hanging on grimly, an empty shot glass in both hands. Apart from the barkeep, who was busy polishing glasses, the only other occupant of the place was a strikingly handsome man sitting alone at a poker table in the corner. His sharply etched face was topped with a full head of gleaming white hair, and a well-greased mustache graced his upper lip. He was playing solitaire.

Stratemeyer ordered a bottle of whiskey and two glasses. With these in hand, he ambled over to the poker table, and the fellow playing solitaire looked up at him.

"Join me in a drink?" Stratemeyer asked pleasantly.

"Never touch it before noon," the man replied.

"Mind if I join you?"

"Sit down. Glad for the company." As he spoke, the fellow deftly gathered up the cards and set them aside. Reaching out his hand, he said, "My name's O'Hare. Brett O'Hare."

"Dean Stratemeyer," the detective said, shaking O'Hare's hand and sitting down across from him.

"Just get in?" O'Hare asked, pleasantly enough.

"Last night."

"Planning on looking for gold, are you?"

"Nope. I'm looking for the Sonora Kid." Stratemeyer watched the man closely as he said it.

"That so?"

"He was heading for Sonora on foot late last night. I'm certain he's holed up in this town somewhere."

O'Hare looked shrewdly at Stratemeyer. "You'd be the fellow that flung himself from the stage and took after the Kid on foot."

Stratemeyer nodded.

"That was a fool thing to do."

"Also unexpected. The Kid had no idea I would do

such a fool thing. Consequently, he was somewhat tardy leaving the area."

As Stratemeyer spoke, he realized that O'Hare was probably one of the few remaining townsmen who was not aware that Stratemeyer had recovered the gold shipment the Sonora Kid had raised from the stage.

Casually, O'Hare said, "Well, more power to you, lawman. You are right. It is the unexpected we must guard ourselves against, and that's the pure truth of it."

A door at the end of the bar opened, and Rafe Barnett emerged. He was in the company of a seedy-looking individual carrying a black leather doctor's bag. The two were engaged in a quiet, intent conversation until Rafe caught sight of Stratemeyer sitting with Brett O'Hare. Startled, Rafe pulled up.

"Just the man I want to see," Stratemeyer called heartily to Rafe.

"Of course. Just a minute," Rafe told him.

Stuffing some folding money in the seedy-looking fellow's breast pocket, he sent the man out of the saloon. Then composing a smile on his cold, narrow face, Rafe Barnett walked over to their table.

"You wanted to see me?" he asked Stratemeyer.

"Yes."

"Stratemeyer, isn't it?" Rafe said cautiously. "Dean Stratemeyer. From the stagecoach. I see you made it back to Sonora."

"More than that." Stratemeyer reached into his pocket and pulled forth a thick envelope. Then with his other hand he reached into his side pocket and lifted out a small sack of gold. He handed both to Rafe. "I believe these were taken from you by the Sonora Kid."

Glancing in some amazement at O'Hare, Rafe reached out and took the money and the gold.

"Thank you, Mr. Stratemeyer. You . . . you were successful then. I must admit, I had no hope at all you would be able to overtake the Sonora Kid on foot."

"As I told O'Hare just now, the Kid had no idea I would do such a fool thing. So he did not move as far and as swiftly as he should have. His other problem was not my doing, however."

"And what was that?" O'Hare asked, an ironic smile playing about his mouth. He seemed to be enjoying an obscure joke.

"His packhorse threw a shoe and went lame."

"But you used it," suggested Rafe, "and followed the Kid?"

"No, the Kid had shot the horse just before I came up behind him, and I had to continue on foot. However, we exchanged shots before he got away, and apparently I succeeded in wounding him. I am quite certain he has lost a considerable quantity of blood."

"Stratemeyer thinks the Kid was able to make it to Sonora," O'Hare told Rafe. "He thinks he might be holed up somewhere in town."

Rafe smiled. "Indeed? Well, Stratemeyer, I thank you for retrieving my fortune—and I wish you luck in finding the Sonora Kid."

Rafe, hoping to conclude their conversation, extended his hand, but Stratemeyer went on. "That man who just left that room with you. He was a doctor, wasn't he?"

"Yes," said Rafe, his voice suddenly cold, his eyes hard. "He is Dr. Miles Wraither. I have some trouble with my stomach since that miserable trip from Stockton. He brought me a bottle of laudanum."

"If you ever have need of him, Mr. Stratemeyer," O'Hare advised pleasantly, "you'll find him in his office above the barbershop. But I must warn you. I would not suggest any reliance on his diagnostic abilities. He purchased his medical kit from an itinerant peddler soon after arriving in California. He knows appallingly little of medicine, but he does have an encyclopedic knowledge of hard liquor. A thoroughly disreputable practitioner, I am afraid."

Stratemeyer nodded pleasantly. "He probably still bleeds his patients, too, I'll bet."

Both men studied his face carefully before trusting

themselves to reply. It was Rafe who spoke first. "Yes," he said. "This doctor, he does."

"He's a real quack," O'Hare contended. He leaned carefully back in his chair. As he did, so, he allowed his frock coat to fall open, revealing a gleaming revolver stuck into his belt. O'Hare smiled at Stratemeyer, then asked, "Would you care for another drink?"

Stratemeyer got to his feet. "No, thank you." He smiled back at O'Hare. "You're right. A drink before noontime can fuddle the senses."

He turned and started from the saloon. As he shouldered his way through the batwings, he forced himself to keep his eyes straight ahead. If he looked back at the two of them, he knew they would see the triumph in his eyes. He had found the Kid. There was no doubt in his mind. No doubt at all. The sorely wounded Sonora Kid was inside that office. As soon as Stratemeyer tracked down the fake sawbones, he would have the added protection of further proof.

Then he would go in after him.

Chapter 5

O' Hare and Rafe watched Stratemeyer until the big man disappeared beyond the batwings. O'Hare was the first to speak.

"He knows, Rafe. That big, easygoing sonofabitch knows who we got in the office, just like it was written all over our faces."

Rafe nodded. "I thought him a fool. Now maybe I think it is me that is the fool. He is like the big clown who always has the last laugh."

"Right now, I figure, he's on his way to find Doc Wraither."

"It will do him no good. Wraither will be able to tell him nothing. I gave him enough to get stinking drunk for a week—maybe even longer."

"Thing is, will Stratemeyer get to him before the liquor does?"

Rafe shrugged. "I do not think so. Wraither was already very drunk when he left here."

"So maybe we got time," O'Hare said, getting to his feet and starting for the office.

José Morales was still on the leather sofa. He appeared to be sleeping peacefully, his head turned to the

61

wall. It had taken the doctor all night to stanch the bleeding, after which he had cauterized the wound with a knife heated by a candle's flame. Then removing José's shirt and tearing it into strips, he bound the unconscious man's torso as tightly as he could manage.

So far, the bleeding had not started up again. There was, however, no good reason for believing that José would live. The slug was still lodged deep in his chest cavity; Wraither had been unwilling to go in after it because, he had insisted, he did not have the needed instruments. And by that time he was already pretty drunk. That was when O'Hare had retreated to the empty saloon and his quiet game of solitaire.

"We've got to get José out of here," Rafe said.

"Sure, but where?"

"To my cabin."

"You have a cabin around here?"

"It is north of here—in the mountains."

"Well, fancy that. And all this time I thought you were living the life of a fine gentleman in San Francisco." O'Hare leaned against the door and crossed his arms.

"Never mind that. This cabin, it is a place of my own. I am the only one who knows of it. You are the second."

"I am flattered."

"We will take José there tonight, as soon as it is dark."

"Assuming our Chicago friend allows us that much leeway."

"He will," snapped Rafe. "I will see to that myself."

Stratemeyer was on his way to Doc Wraither's office when he saw Belle returning to town with Manders. At once he changed direction and was waiting on the hotel porch when Belle alighted from the surrey. Obviously surprised and delighted to see him again, Belle introduced Stratemeyer to Ted Manders. The introductions completed, Stratemeyer told Belle why he wanted to see her. He had some money to return to the young man Prentiss.

"Why, Mr. Stratemeyer!" Belle cried. "You mean you apprehended the Sonora Kid?"

"No, Belle, but I managed to wound him before he got away, and I was able to get back some of what he took from the stage. I do not have your earrings, I am afraid."

"Nevertheless, that's a remarkable accomplishment," said Manders, regarding Stratemeyer with some respect.

"Thank you." He looked back at Belle. "I really would like to find Prentiss. From what I gather, he was counting on this money to become a prospector."

"I am sorry, Mr. Stratemeyer," Belle said, "but I don't even remember seeing him get off the stage. There was a terrible crowd and much confusion. He helped Sharon with her bags, then disappeared."

"Won't you join us in a drink, Mr. Stratemeyer?" Manders inquired. "I would like to hear of your adventures with the Sonora Kid. He's quite a legend around these parts."

Stratemeyer smiled. "Sorry. Perhaps later."

He bid them good-bye and continued down the street. The barbershop was easy enough to find, and Stratemeyer knew the doctor's office was just above it. After climbing the wooden steps to the second story, he knocked on the door. There was no answer. He tried the door and found it open. Entering, he called out a second time. Still no response. He closed the door behind him and looked around.

He was standing in one of two adjoining rooms. It was obvious to Stratemeyer that the place served the doctor as an office and as living quarters. A strong smell, compounded of carbolic acid and raw whiskey, hung in the air and made Stratemeyer's stomach move queasily. The single window was shut tightly. Taking it upon himself to open it, he drew back the curtains, loosing into the fetid atmosphere a choking cloud of dust. Persisting grimly, he flung open the window and tied back the curtains. At once a powerful beam of sunlight sliced through the gloom, revealing with disheartening clarity the awful shambles of the place. He had intruded into what seemed to be the den of a sick animal.

At that moment he heard a movement behind him as someone came out of the adjoining room. He was in the act of turning when what felt like the barrel of a six-gun crashed down onto the top of his skull with the force of a pile driver.

He was unconscious before he struck the floor.

Sharon Cortland was exhausted, but not so much from the long day's wagon ride with Jim Coleman as from the tension brought by her search for Tim. Just knowing that he might be nearby caused Sharon to remain constantly alert, noticing every unusual sound or movement in her surroundings. Because of this unflagging attention to the landscape, Sharon had had a change of heart. Her wish to flee this hurried, wild country had vanished entirely. As she finished preparing her bedroll upon the fragrant pine needles and sat back to contemplate the forest night, she shook her head in wonderment, realizing just how much she had begun to love this grand, rugged country.

On the stagecoach ride from Stockton, the small coach window had constricted her view of the wilderness through which she was traveling, fragmenting it. Today, however, she had been able to take in at one glance the astonishing vistas that greeted her on almost every turn.

The wondrous, unobstructed view had even been enough to make her forget Jim Coleman's oppressive nearness. He had driven the wagon at a stolid pace that had at first irritated her. Soon, however, she had grown to appreciate it. As they climbed ever higher, she kept glimpsing spectacular vistas, vaulting, snow-tipped crags—all of it on a scale that first filled her with awe, then with a humility she had never felt before.

And the trees! She had been used to big trees in Maine. But these were not trees; they were monuments. So high did some of them tower, she was almost convinced they brushed the clouds that scudded above them. It was plain that out here, far from the filthy towns and the noisome, squalid men who caroused there, she had found a truly virgin wilderness, its pristine stillness unbroken by the echoing bite of the ax, its scented earth not yet violated by the ripping, heedless plow.

Leaning her head back against a small tree, she gazed up at the sky. From this height, the stars were startling in their brilliant profusion. Never had she seen such a display. As she watched, she glimpsed a shooting star—and made a wish. It had to do with finding Tim, of course. Taking a deep breath, she added a silent prayer to her wish. Her soul quieted by this heartfelt benediction, she unbuttoned her high shoes and crawled carefully into her bedroll.

In a surprising gesture, Jim Coleman had provided Sharon with a coarsely woven bedroll made out of two large blankets sewn together. He had presented it to her after she had returned from the stream where she had been cleaning the pots and pans used in making their supper. It was in appreciation of the delicious meal she had prepared over the open fire, he had explained. She had been surprised at the gusto with which he wolfed down the pan-fried beans and salt pork. Later, however, as if to make up for having complimented her so effusively, Coleman mentioned that he hoped her morning coffee would be stronger than the coffee she had made for supper. To that she had readily agreed. Anything to keep the man happy.

Pulling a flap of the bedroll up over her shoulder, she turned to face the wagon, which was down the slope. The four horses were dim shadows grazing in a meadow farther below. The campfire's embers glowed in the darkness, giving off a surprising amount of light. She sought out Jim Coleman's reclining form, and once she spied it beside the wagon, she relaxed and closed her eyes.

In a moment she was asleep.

Something ugly and obscene was coiled around Sharon.

She struggled in a violent, desperate effort to escape the nightmare, but awakening in a cold sweat, she found herself still held within the constricting coils. Uttering a tiny, terrified scream, she twisted wildly, futilely.

For a second or two she thought it was the entangled bedroll that held her. Then she felt Jim Coleman's hot, unpleasant breath as he struggled to hold her. She screamed again as he pushed his face close and tried to fasten his lips over hers. Snapping viciously, she sank her teeth in his lips. Coleman cried out and pulled away. The sickly sweet warmth of Coleman's blood on her lips disgusted her, but she did not let it prevent her from continuing her efforts to get free. Yet Coleman had the advantage—he was stronger than she, and he was inside the bedroll with her!

She felt his sweating body pressing eagerly against hers as he thrust a knee between her legs and moved it relentlessly upward, forcing her to spread her thighs. In a choking sob of terror she cried out—to the stars, to God, to anyone—for help.

Lifting momentarily from her, Coleman slapped her face hard. "Damn you, shut up!" he cried through his bloody lips. "You know goddam well this is what you want, bitch!"

"No!" Sharon screamed through stinging tears.

He slapped her again. "Lie still, I said!"

She managed then to free one hand. Reaching up she grabbed his hair and yanked back with all her might. Grunting in pain, he reached back and caught her wrist in a viselike clamp so painful it caused her to release her grip. With a mean chuckle of triumph, Coleman pinned her arms and drove his knee still farther up between her thighs.

Suddenly there were two forms struggling over her!

The second one swore violently at Coleman and ripped the bedroll from his back. Coleman reached up to ward off a blow, but was struck viciously anyway and went tumbling halfway down the slope, the second man following after him.

Sitting up, her heart thudding in her throat like a wild thing, she watched in growing amazement as Dan Prentiss caught up with Coleman and the two began slugging it out, toe to toe. That her savior was Dan Prentiss she had no doubt. When he swore, she had recognized his voice. Dan must have followed them all the way from Sonora.

The two struggling men had reached the wagon by this time, their brawling, vicious battle continuing. Sharon wanted to help and started hesitantly down the slope until she realized that her nightgown had been ripped clear up to her waist. Halting in some confusion as she quickly wound the torn gown about her, she watched the two men battling below her. Dan was punching Coleman now with continuous, sledging blows that eventually drove him to the ground.

Dan stepped back. Coleman was on his hands and knees, his head sagging almost to the ground. He looked thoroughly and miserably beaten. Sharon was relieved to see Dan turn away from Coleman and start back up the slope toward her.

"Are you all right, Sharon?" he called to her as he caught sight of her standing in the moonlight.

"I'm fine," she told him shakily. "But where on earth did you come from?"

He was about to answer when a shot rang out from the slope below him. Dan staggered, then slumped forward onto the slope. Coleman had taken a gun from his gear by the wagon and shot Dan!

She plunged down the slope to Dan's side and rolled him over. "Dan!" she cried.

Grimacing up at her, he moaned, "Damn Coleman's hide! Where is he?"

"I'm right here, you sonofabitch!" Coleman snarled, looming over them both, a huge revolver clutched in his right hand. "And I'm going to finish you right now!"

With a wild screech of rage, Sharon flung herself at Coleman. The force of her charge flung him backward down the slope. She felt his legs tangle with hers, and the two of them went down heavily, the full weight of her body crashing down upon his. With a grunt, the air exploded from Coleman's lungs.

Coleman rolled over and tried to crawl away from her. But Sharon reached under him and managed to get a grip on the barrel of his revolver. Coleman twisted viciously and yanked the gun away from her—and it went off! The force of its detonation appeared to lift Coleman off the ground. She heard him groan with terror and pain as he went limp beneath her. Grimly, she rolled him over and snatched up the weapon. Coleman was still alive, whimpering.

She stood up. With both hands aiming the revolver down at Coleman, Sharon pulled the trigger.

Incredibly, she missed. But as the round plunged into the ground beside Coleman, he leaped to his feet. Holding on to his right side, he plunged frantically down the slope. Still beside herself with rage, Sharon managed to steady her aim with both hands and get off a second shot. She did not know if this round struck Coleman, for a moment later the fleeing man was swallowed up in darkness.

Flinging down the weapon, she turned and bolted back up the slope to where Dan Prentiss still lay.

It was dark, pitch dark. The shadowy form bending over Stratemeyer smelled like the chief demon in a whiskey hell. The rest were blasting a tunnel through the back of his head. Stratemeyer groaned and tried to move. The shadow pulled away, weaving unsteadily in the awful darkness of the place.

"Who the hell are you, mister?" the shadow inquired.

"I might ask you the same question," Stratemeyer managed, attempting to sit up.

"You're in my office, so I got a right to ask you. Besides, it's after office hours and the office is closed."

"You'd be Doc Wraither then."

"That's me."

"The door was open so I walked in to wait for you."
Stratemeyer pulled himself blindly onto a chair that had
been protruding into his back.

He heard Wraither stumbling in the dark as he moved
away. A moment later a sulfur match flared, and the
doctor lit a lamp on his desk. From the way his hand
shook, Stratemeyer assumed the man was very drunk, and
indeed, slumping into a chair by his desk, Wraither placed
a fresh bottle of whiskey down on it. He produced two
filthy glasses from a drawer, filled one, and downed its
contents. Then he nodded toward Stratemeyer.

"Maybe you could use some of this."

"Maybe I could."

"You better pour then."

Moving carefully so as not to shake his brains loose,
Stratemeyer reached for the bottle and the glass. Filling
the glass halfway, he downed the drink as quickly as he
had poured it.

"Thank you," he said, as the cheap whiskey slammed
down his throat and struck his stomach like grapeshot.
"That's really fine stuff."

"It don't need to be fancy to get you where you want
to go."

"Guess not. I'm Dean Stratemeyer."

"I knew that when I lit the lamp. Saw you when I left
the Gold Nugget this morning."

"What time is it now?"

"Close on to midnight."

"You don't keep very good hours."

"I ain't a very good doctor."

"Could I have some more of that whiskey?"

"Help yourself," Wraither said. But he didn't sound
all that eager to let Stratemeyer lighten the bottle.

This time Stratemeyer drank the whiskey with a bit
more caution.

"You look bad," Wraither said, taking back the bottle
and pouring himself another tumblerful. "You come to
me for medical help?"

"I look bad because you—or someone you know—

struck me over the head with a six-gun." Stratemeyer felt the top of his head. There was a sizable bump, and he winced as he probed it.

"It wasn't me," Wraither said, gulping his whiskey.

"Then one of your friends. I'm thinking it was Brett O'Hare or Rafe Barnett."

Wraither shrugged. "You got trouble with them, it ain't my concern."

"How come you were at the Gold Nugget?"

"I drink there."

"In the owner's office?"

Wraither shrugged again.

"You were treating someone. Who was it?"

"I don't think I remember."

"Was it Rafe Barnett?"

"Yeah. That's right. It was Rafe."

"What was wrong with him?"

"He . . . he had a headache."

"That's funny. He told me it was a stomachache. Don't you know the difference?"

"Sure, I know the difference. I just forgot. He did have a stomachache. A bad one."

Stratemeyer reached for the bottle. He smiled. "I think I am going to have to empty this bottle on the floor."

"Hey!" Wraither cried, reaching out. "Don't do that!"

"You were tending to a wounded man in that office, weren't you?"

"All right! So I was! What business is that of yours? Give me back that bottle."

Stratemeyer placed the whiskey down on the doctor's cluttered desk. "Tell me about the wounded man."

"There ain't anything to tell. He was wounded."

"Shot in the back, was he?"

"That's right."

"A round from a revolver, would you say—or a rifle?"

"Revolver."

"A young Mexican, about eighteen?"

Wraither filled his glass. His shaking was getting worse. "Yeah," he said. "That's him, all right."

"How bad is he?"

"He won't live, if that's what you mean."

"You couldn't get the bullet out?"

"Didn't try. I didn't have my instruments with me. Like I said, I was in there for a nightcap and they got me to tend to this wounded fellow."

"Last night was it?"

"Yeah. I worked on him all night. I was so tired I been sleeping all this time at my lady friend's place."

"Do you know who that wounded Mexican was?"

"No."

"The Sonora Kid."

"Shit. That blow on your head must've really scrambled your brains. You want me to look at it?"

Slowly, carefully, Stratemeyer got to his feet. "My hat's around here somewhere," he said.

The doctor found it on the floor and handed it to the detective. The crown was bent where the gun barrel had crunched down on it. Pushing out the dent, Stratemeyer carefully placed his hat back on, then headed for the door. When he reached it, he looked back at Wraither.

"I might have to call you as a witness pretty soon. Don't go anywhere."

"Now where the hell would I go, mister?" He held up the glass of whiskey and saluted Stratemeyer. "I got me a home here."

Stratemeyer pulled open the door and left the place. In his shaky condition, the steep stairway was a challenge, but he managed it without mishap and proceeded through the dark, noisy streets toward the Gold Nugget.

He was too late, he knew. The Sonora Kid must long since have been spirited away from the saloon. That was why Stratemeyer's unknown assailant had tried to drive a gun barrel through his head. The blow had been meant to kill him, Stratemeyer had no doubt. But once again his thick skull had saved him.

During the time he was unconscious, they could have taken the Kid anywhere, but if Wraither was right, that didn't really matter any more. The Kid was a dead man. He would rob no more stages.

Nevertheless, there was one question Stratemeyer still needed answering. Why were Brett O'Hare and Rafe Barnett mixed up with a notorious highwayman?

Reaching the Gold Nugget, Stratemeyer strode in and shouldered his way up to the bar. He beckoned to the barkeep.

"I'd like to speak to O'Hare," Stratemeyer told him.

"He's gone."

"For the night?"

The barkeep nodded carefully.

"What about his friend?"

"Rafe?"

Stratemeyer nodded.

"He's gone, too."

"All night?"

"Reckon so."

"Does that mean you're in charge?"

"It does."

"Do you know when they'll be back?"

"When they get back."

Stratemeyer's patience was running out. "Got any idea where I can find the sheriff in this town?"

"Sure have. He's right over there at that table in the corner."

Stratemeyer turned. He saw a puffy-faced inebriate with bushy eyebrows and shaggy gray hair. If this was the sheriff, he appeared to be in very poor condition.

Glancing back at the barkeep, Stratemeyer asked, "Does he have a name?"

"Mike Emory."

"What's he doing in here? Where's his office?"

The barkeep chuckled. "Why, right here in the Gold Nugget. Mr. O'Hare likes to have him around. Keeps out the rowdies. Sheriff Emory likes it here, too. We take very good care of him."

Stratemeyer understood perfectly. He looked back at the sheriff, who was brooding over his glass. If the time had come for a waiting game, maybe Stratemeyer should wait with a sheriff who was evidently in O'Hare's pay—and who probably knew a hell of a lot more than he was supposed to know.

Purchasing a bottle from the barkeep, Stratemeyer headed for the sheriff's table to make his acquaintance.

Chapter 6

No, Sharon's eyes were not playing tricks on her. She was certain now. It really *was* a small covered wagon moving across the field below the trail. As near as she could make out, two men were on the front seat. Surely, if she could attract their attention, they would be willing to help!

Up all night in an effort to stanch the wound in Dan's thigh, she had just made another futile attempt to boost him up onto the wagon seat. Once again, too weak to help, Dan had collapsed back to the ground and now lay semiconscious on the grass beside the wagon.

"Dan!" she exclaimed excitedly. "There's a wagon crossing that field, and two men are in it! They'll help us, I'm sure!"

Dan muttered something unintelligible and tried to get to his feet.

"No," she commanded. "Lie still. I'll get them."

She ran to the edge of the roadway and called down to the wagon. But the men driving it did not even slow down. She was too far away, she realized. They could not possibly hear her at this distance. Plunging down the slope, she yelled and waved her arms frantically. This time she caught their attention, and the wagon halted. One of the two men, who now turned in her direction, stood up and shaded his eyes.

Scrambling to a halt, Sharon waved again, calling for help with all the force her lungs could muster. The fellow shading his eyes jumped down from the wagon and started across the meadow toward her. Enormously relieved, she brushed a damp strand of hair from her eyes as she progressed down the slope at a less frantic pace to meet the fellow. Abruptly, however, he stopped and turned back toward his companion, still on the wagon seat. After what appeared to be a short discussion, he returned to the wagon and climbed back up onto his seat. At once the wagon jerked into motion and continued on across the meadow.

For a moment Sharon refused to believe it.

Then, uttering a small cry of fury, she plunged on down the slope, crying out to them repeatedly, pleading with them to wait. But only when she broke out of the timber at the foot of the slope and started across the meadow after them did the driver of the team finally give in and halt the wagon a second time.

As she raced across the meadow toward the wagon, the two men maintained their positions, simply waiting for her to reach them. Only when she was within a few yards of the wagon did Sharon realize that the driver was Rafe Barnett, her fellow passenger on the stagecoach, the one who had kept so quiet next to Stratemeyer.

Scrambling up at last before them, exhausted from her long run and furious at their apparent unwillingness to help, she told Rafe angrily, "I need help, Mr. Barnett! A man's been wounded."

"Pleased to meet you again, Miss Cortland," Barnett said coldly. "I am sorry you have this trouble. But we have urgent business of our own."

"Is it urgent enough for you to abandon one of your fellow passengers? Dan Prentiss has been shot!"

Barnett sighed. "It is a small world indeed, Miss

Cortland. But I have just told you. My business, it is urgent, too."

"Don't you see? Dan will die if he doesn't get help soon. What kind of man are you, Mr. Barnett?"

The fellow sitting beside Barnett smiled and touched the brim of his hat to Sharon. In his early thirties, he was a sharp contrast to Barnett—much taller, with hollow cheeks, gleaming white hair and a coal-black mustache.

"My name is Brett O'Hare, ma'am," he explained. "Since Rafe here don't seem inclined to introduce us, who might you be?"

"Sharon Cortland," she snapped impatiently. "Now, *will* you help us?"

"Of course we are going to help you ma'am," O'Hare told her. "Get up beside us and we will be most happy to take you back to your wounded friend." He turned to his companion. "Ain't that so, Rafe?"

Rafe Barnett was obviously furious that his partner was yielding, but he controlled his anger, offering no argument as Sharon climbed wearily up onto the seat beside O'Hare. In his flat, emotionless voice, he asked Sharon where she had left Dan. When she told him, he turned the horses and headed back to the roadway.

As they rode, O'Hare asked Sharon exactly what had happened, and she told them. At the moment she revealed Jim Coleman's role in the miserable tale, she thought she detected a sudden flare of interest in Rafe Barnett. But she could not be sure, since the man was so taciturn.

Arriving back at the wagon where she had left Dan, Sharon was dismayed to see that he was completely unconscious. Jumping down from her seat, she rushed to his side. O'Hare followed close behind her and bent down on one knee to examine Dan's thigh wound.

"The bullet's gone through, Miss Cortland, but it looks like he's lost a lot of blood."

"I know. I tried to stop it."

"Take off his shirt and tear it into strips," O'Hare told her. Then he stood up and walked back to the wagon. Something in O'Hare's voice calmed Sharon. She promptly did as he bid, and as soon as she had fashioned the strips, he took them from her. Producing a fifth of whiskey from the wagon, he saturated a strip and pressed it tightly against the still-flowing wound.

"Hold it against there tightly," O'Hare told her.

Again she did as she was told, holding the compress in place against the wound until O'Hare had bound it with another strip. The compress now secure, she leaned back and watched as O'Hare wound the remaining strips as tightly as he could around Dan's thigh.

She was pleased to see no sign of blood seeping through the bandages. O'Hare had indeed stopped the bleeding.

"Thank you," Sharon said to O'Hare, as the two stood up.

Rafe Barnett moved closer then, his cold eyes studying Sharon closely. "You told us that Jim Coleman shot Prentiss. And that you shot Coleman. Where is Coleman now? How badly is he hurt?"

"I don't know," she told him. "He ran off."

"But you *did* hit him?"

"We struggled for the gun. It went off and wounded him. I am sure of it."

Rafe looked about the slopes and timbered hillsides surrounding them, his eyes curiously alight. "Then he is around here somewhere, hurt."

"I am afraid so."

O'Hare touched the brim of his hat to Sharon. "Guess you'll be all right now," he said. "We'll be moving on."

"But what do you mean?" Sharon cried. "You can't leave us here like this! Dan still has a severe wound. He's lost so much blood he's unconscious! We've *got* to get him back to Sonora."

"Then take him," Barnett said.

"But *you* must! Your wagon has a canvas. He'll be protected, and you can do it in much less time than it would take me with this huge freight wagon."

"Are you serious, ma'am?" O'Hare inquired politely.

"You mean you want us to turn around and take Prentiss back to Sonora?"

"Yes," Sharon said. Then she added, "Either that or let me use your wagon to take him back."

"And what do you propose we do with Coleman's goods here?"

"Take them on to the Pine Hill diggings."

The two men looked at each other, obviously astonished at Sharon's temerity. With a trace of amusement in his eyes, O'Hare cleared his throat and said, "I am afraid that is out of the question, ma'am. Like Rafe said back there, we got other business."

"Urgent business," emphasized Barnett.

"What is more urgent than saving a dying man?"

"Now that ain't a sure thing," O'Hare said, shrugging. "He might not die."

"But there is a chance he will die if we don't get him back to Sonora. Isn't that true?"

"Ma'am," O'Hare said in some exasperation, "the only doctor we got in Sonora would be no help at all."

"I don't believe you. And if you do not help me, I will let everyone in Pine Hill and Sonora know that you two abandoned a dying man—because of your urgent business!"

Barnett took O'Hare's arm and drew him away from Sharon. Retreating as far as their wagon, they had a short, animated discussion. Sharon could not hear a word, but she had no doubt that they were taking seriously her threat to expose their callousness. She watched them, fuming. Surely, Dan's life was more important than any business they might have out here in this wilderness. And she did not believe for one minute O'Hare's glib assertion that the Sonora physician would be of no help.

The two men paced back to Sharon. O'Hare, watching her with amused curiosity, kept in the background as this time Barnett did all the talking.

"We take Prentiss then. And you will go to Pine Hill. Your brother, he is at the diggings there?"

"That is what I heard. Of course, I am not sure he is still there."

Barnett nodded patiently, almost as if he were dealing with a stubborn and willful child. "But you think he still is there. Is that not so?"

"It is."

"And you want much to join your brother."

"Of course."

"I have a cabin not far from here." He glanced down at the man lying unconscious at their feet. "I have seen such wounds before. O'Hare and I, we will take good care of Prentiss. When he is well, we will bring him back to Sonora with us, all right?"

Sharon was keenly disappointed. This was not what she wanted. "You won't take him back now?"

Barnett smiled. But there was steel in the smile, and Sharon felt a sudden chill run up her spine.

"No," Barnett said. "We have just told you. There is no help for your friend in Sonora. We will take care of him. And you will go on to Pine Hill. We will do it this way, Miss Cortland, and you will not have to spread lies about us. Is that not a fine solution?"

"You won't let me take him back in your wagon?"

"No."

At that moment Prentiss stirred fitfully and groaned. The three of them turned quickly and looked down at him. In that instant, Sharon saw that she really had no choice. All she could do was agree to Barnett's plan.

"All right," she said reluctantly. "But please be careful with him. He . . . he saved my life."

O'Hare stepped forward then, a sudden smile on his lean face. "Of course we will, Miss Cortland. So don't you worry. He'll be up and about in no time."

"If he lives." Barnett spoke sharply, and this time his glance cut through Sharon like a cold knife.

"No need for that kind of talk," O'Hare said bluntly to his partner, a sudden edge to his voice. "Now give me a hand with him."

Stepping back, Sharon watched as the two men lifted Dan between them and carried him over to the wagon. Jumping up onto the tailgate, O'Hare pulled the barely con-

scious Prentiss swiftly in after him. Sharon hurried over to
the wagon to make sure Dan was all right, but at that
moment Barnett moved his body just enough to block her
view. O'Hare emerged from the wagon then, jumped
down, flung up the tailgate, and secured it.

Smiling at Sharon, he said, "Dan's got a fever, all
right. But that's to be expected."

Still apprehensive, Sharon simply nodded. Something
was wrong about these two men. She suddenly had the
awful feeling that in her haste to get help for Dan, she
might have succeeded only in injuring him further. But
what other course of action could she have pursued? As
Barnett had just pointed out to her in his cold way, her
job now was to deliver Coleman's wagon to the Pine Hill
diggings and seek out her brother.

Yes, she thought wearily. First things first. It was
Tim she had come all this way to find—and she would just
have to pray that Dan would survive and that these two
men would do as they promised.

"Thank you," she said, her earlier anger draining
from her. "I guess I'd better get going then."

O'Hare walked with her to Coleman's wagon. "Coleman
didn't hurry much yesterday, did he, Miss Cortland?"

"Why, what do you mean?"

"He could have made the trip from Sonora in one
day. There's less than five miles for you to go. And all you
covered yesterday was ten. Usually, it is a one day trip
from Sonora, even with a freight wagon this heavily loaded."

Sharon knew at once what O'Hare was trying to tell
her. With some bitterness, she asked, "When did you two
leave Sonora?"

"Last night."

"I see," she said grimly. "It took you only one night's
ride to come this far. Then it is quite obvious Mr. Coleman took advantage of my ignorance."

"That's what it looks like, ma'am."

Sharon took a deep breath, and in a sudden, terrible
burst of anger, she told O'Hare, "I know how this must
sound, Mr. O'Hare. But I don't care what happens to that

man. It is a terrible thing to contemplate—the death of a fellow man. But if Jim Coleman were to die, I would not lose a minute's sleep."

Barnett moved alongside O'Hare, his dark face expressing rare enthusiasm. "I agree with you, Miss Cortland," he said, his eyes gleaming. "A man without honor does not deserve to live. You did the right thing to shoot this one. A woman's honor is worth any man's life."

"Why thank you, Mr. Barnett. Thank you for saying that."

The horses, which Sharon had harnessed first thing that morning, stood waiting. When she turned to climb up onto the seat, O'Hare stepped quickly forward to help her, then handed her the reins. She took them from him, and the two men stepped back and smiled up at her. Rafe Barnett's words had made her feel much better about the man. Perhaps she had taken his taciturn nature the wrong way. It was certainly likely that he and his partner would take good care of Dan. After all, O'Hare had already stanched Dan's wound, succeeding where she had failed.

She gathered up the reins and called sharply to the four-horse team, their patient bodies surging forward with sudden purpose. The wagon creaked, the wheels dug into the soft ground, and at once she was moving up the trail. Looking back at O'Hare and Barnett, she called out goodbye and thanks.

Stepping back, they waved to her.

It was not long before the awful fury that had caused her to speak of Jim Coleman with such utter lack of charity left her shaken and penitent. What she had said to O'Hare was close to blasphemy. No matter how evil Jim Coleman was, in the eyes of God he was still one of His children. The devil himself must have put those terrible words into her mouth—the devil and her awful fatigue. After all, she had been up all the night before.

She shook her head impatiently. Being tired was no excuse. If Jim Coleman were to die of the gunshot wound suffered at her hands, she would never be able to forgive herself—not entirely, that is. There was no excuse for taking the life of a fellow human being, and Sharon was profoundly sorry for what she had said. She hoped God would understand and forgive her—just as someday He would have to understand and forgive the likes of Jim Coleman.

Feeling a little better about herself, Sharon turned her attention to the team and with considerable spirit shouted "Giddap!" It was a steep climb, and they were struggling some. At the sound of her shrill command, the four horses bowed their heads and increased their efforts, the leather harnesses squeaking as the beasts strained against them.

Some time later, when the wagon reached a level stretch, Sharon pulled up to rest the team. Tying the heavy reins around the brake handle, she took a deep breath and looked down at the meadow in hopes of glimpsing O'Hare and Barnett's wagon. She experienced some difficulty at first in picking it out, and when she did at last, the wagon was no larger than a tiny dot moving almost imperceptibly into a distant pass.

Beyond the pass she glimpsed a narrow valley. Guarding its entrance was a steep, beetling cliff, on top of which stood a single towering pine, which must once have been struck by a lightning bolt. Barren of branches and as white as marble, it looked like an enormous flagpole.

Even as she watched, Barnett's wagon disappeared beyond the pass. With a sigh, she untied the reins and started her horses moving once again. As the freight wagon creaked forward, the shoulder of a mountain obscured her view of the valley and its gleaming white sentinel. All thought of Dan Prentiss left her mind at last as she concentrated on keeping her heavily laden wagon on the road.

With all her heart she hoped that O'Hare was right— that it would not be long before she was in sight of the Pine Hill diggings. She was tired, deathly tired. But she knew that the sight of her brother's face would revive her as could nothing else in all this world.

*   *   *

As Rafe entered the valley, he was careful not to look at the mountain slope to his right. Resting precariously on a level spot a few hundred yards up the heavily forested slope was a man-sized boulder, which Rafe himself had levered into place. The boulder served not only as a marker for Rafe's mine, but also as an effective device for hiding its entrance. The gold he had taken from his mine this past year had enabled Rafe to purchase the Gold Nugget. And he did not intend to share with a single gringo—or anyone else, for that matter—the vein of gold-bearing quartz he had uncovered deep within the mountain's flank. Already, to keep for himself the secret of his mine, he had killed two gringos—and he would not hesitate to kill more.

Watching O'Hare covertly as they entered the valley, Rafe saw that he did not appear even to notice the boulder. Rafe relaxed, chiding himself. It had been almost impossible for him not to stare at the boulder the moment it came within view. As the source of his wealth, how could it be otherwise? For O'Hare, of course, it was simply one more feature of the landscape, no more noticeable than any other.

They came to Rafe's cabin. It was a small, rude affair with unpainted planking for the roof and rough-cut logs for sides. The door hung on leather hinges, and the windows were covered with oiled paper. Climbing down from the wagon seat, Rafe stretched himself wearily as O'Hare went around to the rear of the wagon and let down the tailgate.

"Rafe . . ." O'Hare called softly.

Rafe hurried around to the rear of the wagon.

"José's dead," O'Hare said.

Nodding grimly, Rafe stepped past O'Hare and looked in. In the pale light filtering through the canvas, Rafe saw José's cold, almost bluish features staring up at him from the floor of the wagon. It was only the husk of his friend, Rafe realized, nothing more. José's reckless young spirit had long since left this miserable scene. For a brief, melancholy moment, Rafe found himself wondering when exactly it had taken leave of José. Could it have been while they were wrangling with that fool woman about Prentiss?

He took a deep, weary breath and stepped back from the wagon. He glanced at O'Hare. "And the other one?"

"He's running a fever, but he's still alive."

"Damn," Rafe said bitterly. "José dies, but this fool of a gringo lives."

"Blame Stratemeyer for that, Rafe."

"Yes. I intend to do that. For a fat, slow-moving gringo, he has already done much damage. I shall have to deal with him when I get back."

"So what do we do now?" O'Hare said.

"We bury José. What else do you think?" Rafe snapped.

"And Prentiss?"

"We will tend to him later. After we have given José a proper burial."

O'Hare nodded. Then he peered closely at Rafe, the faintest suggestion of a smile playing about his mouth. "By the way, Rafe," he said, almost gently, "have you given consideration to the fact that I also am a gringo?"

Rafe looked with sudden surprise at O'Hare. Then he laughed, shortly, bitterly. "But you are not a fat gringo, and you do not move slowly."

"Glad to hear you say that."

"There is a shovel in the cabin," Rafe said, turning abruptly to lead the way.

Two hours later José was in his final resting place, and as O'Hare looked up from the fresh mound of earth and gazed out over the valley, he found he liked very much this small, hidden place of Rafe's. No wonder Rafe had kept it a secret.

"Bow your head, O'Hare," Rafe told him.

Obediently, O'Hare did so, and Rafe prayed in Spanish. Only a few of the words did O'Hare understand, but he kept his head bowed dutifully. Abruptly, Rafe broke into English.

". . . Mother of God, hear me. I swear to you on Josita's grave that José will be avenged. And that I will continue to punish Josita's murderers as well. I will wear the black hood in place of José and will not rest until her vengeance has been completed. Hear me, Mother of God. Hear me, too, Satan. I swear it to you, as well. Heaven or hell. It is all the same to me."

Rafe raised his head, scanned the valley one time, then walked past O'Hare, his eyes as bleak as O'Hare had ever remembered seeing them. Shrugging, O'Hare picked up both shovels and, resting them on his shoulders, began tramping down the path that led from this small clearing.

Rafe paused by the grave a moment longer, looking farther up the slope to where the huge boulder blocked the entrance of his mine. Satisfied that O'Hare suspected nothing and that his gold remained undiscovered, he turned in the opposite direction toward the cabin and followed his white-haired companion.

Prentiss was raving slightly when O'Hare peered into the wagon to check on his condition. Glancing down at the thigh wound, he saw that the bandage had darkened considerably. The stubborn wound had broken open again. O'Hare leaned into the wagon and rested his palm on Prentiss's forehead; he whistled softly.

Rafe, who had saddled one of the horses when he returned from burying José, swung into the saddle now and kneed his mount closer.

"Prentiss is bad, no?"

"Bad enough."

"He will be dead soon?"

"Unless we can clean out that wound." Backing out of the wagon, O'Hare turned and squinted up at Rafe. "The bullet went clear through, but it ripped open an artery and tore him up pretty bad, looks like. We better carry him into the cabin and cauterize the wound."

"No. Kill him and bury him beside José."

"Kill him? Just like that?"

"He is in pain. He has a fever. To cauterize the wound would not help, I think. He has lost too much blood. We have no skill to save him."

"That ain't what you told that pretty blonde."

"I would tell her anything to be rid of her. Or did you want her to look into the wagon and see José?"

Rafe pulled his horse around impatiently.

"Where the hell are you going?" O'Hare asked.

"That is my business. If that woman speaks the truth, I will return soon enough. Bury Prentiss before I come back. We do not have much time."

"Dammit, Rafe! Why are you so all-fired anxious to bury him?"

Rafe looked coldly down at O'Hare. "Why is it you do not see? If Prentiss survives, he will know of this valley. And soon everyone will know of this valley. José's grave will be found. Alive, this Prentiss is a problem for us. Dead, he is in God's hands. Like José, he will suffer no more. Do it, O'Hare. Kill him."

Clapping his spurs to his mount's flanks, Rafe lifted it to a sudden gallop.

For a long moment O'Hare watched Rafe ride back out of the valley. O'Hare knew his partner well enough to know that if he didn't take care of this chore before Rafe returned, Rafe would do it himself and would be angry with O'Hare besides. With a weary shrug, he grabbed Prentiss's shirt and pulled him around so that his head was resting on the tailgate. Satisfied that he had a clearer view of his target, O'Hare eased his Colt out of his belt, cocked it, and aimed carefully at a spot just behind Prentiss's left ear.

Chapter 7

T he day before, when Belle had visited Ted Manders's mine, he had been so impressed by her interest in its operation that he had asked his new lady friend to accompany him again today. Belle had readily agreed but not because the mine itself intrigued her—its owner she found much more fascinating.

Now looking down once again at the plundered riverbed, Belle winced at the sound of gravel being dumped into the whirling trommels. She wondered if she could ever get used to such a tearing, grating sound. How on earth could those poor men down there stand it?

Then she caught sight of Manders. He was leaving his foreman and was on his way to the footpath. During the ride to the mine he had seemed preoccupied. Now the discouraged set of his shoulders as he climbed up to her was more proof, if such were needed, that all was not going well.

"Tell me, Ted," she said, as soon as he approached her. "What's wrong? I want to know."

He stopped in surprise. "Why, Belle, nothing is wrong!"

"You mean you refuse to tell me?" Her arms were

crossed, and one corner of her mouth drew up into a knowing smirk.

He looked at her for a long moment, then sighed. "Later, Belle. I'll tell you later, and that's a promise. But I have other plans for this day. My petty troubles can wait, but this lovely day will not. So let us enjoy it as we had planned."

Belle knew enough not to press the issue. And in truth, it was a lovely day. The pine-scented air was bright with sunshine and filled with midsummer music: the wind in the pines, the cheerful call of the birds, the refreshing sound of rushing water. A perfect day for a picnic—which was just what they had in mind. Manders had told her of a spot where they could look down on the valley and see all of Sonora. From that distance, he had promised her with a laugh, they would hear none of the grating sounds that were bothering her here.

They climbed into the surrey and left the mine, Manders setting the blacks to a nice trot. Though he tried to keep up the light conversation, he soon lapsed into preoccupied silence. Accepting this philosophically, Belle leaned back, welcoming this chance to collect her own thoughts. She too was troubled somewhat, but her worry stemmed from the course her life had taken since meeting Ted Manders . . . or at least the speed with which the two of them had come together. A woman with passions as natural and as powerful as her companion's, she knew full well what Manders intended in the privacy of the wilderness after their picnic was done. For her part, the prospect was a pleasing one. She could not even contemplate it without that inevitable rush of heat that seemed to consume her entire body. It had been so long . . .

But that was biology. There were other things to consider as well. For one thing, that such a man as Ted Manders should be unattached was a magnificent stroke of luck—or a lie. And Belle was inclined to believe it was the latter. Somewhere back east, she was sure, Manders had a wife . . . perhaps even children. This little tryst in the wilderness of California was what they both needed, obviously, but there was little likelihood it could lead to anything more enduring.

Her problem now, as she saw it, was whether or not to broach this unpleasant topic with Manders while on this outing. It could only bring discord, and that most assuredly was not what she wanted. Furthermore, from the melancholy cast that had now fallen over Manders's features, she realized that such a topic—added to his other preoccupations concerning the mine—would simply turn this afternoon into an unpleasant trial for him. He had treated her too kindly for her to spoil things in such a fashion.

As Belle came to this decision, she took a deep breath and relaxed, resolving to do what she could to make this a memorable occasion for both of them. Life, as she well knew, provided precious few such moments for one to look back upon and cherish.

She would not cheat either of them of that.

As Manders pulled the blacks to a halt, he smiled at her with his old hearty cheer, took her hand, and helped her down.

"Wait'll you see it," he told her. "It'll take your breath away."

A moment later, she did indeed experience the awe and excitement he obviously felt. Soaring, timber-topped cliffs loomed over them on both sides, and it was through this magnificent portal that they glimpsed the golden hills and sweeping mountains that extended in stupendous ranks for miles. The foothills came first, then the smaller mountains, and finally the towering, jagged peaks, the entire range bathed in a smoky, purplish haze.

Just below them lay the town of Sonora, a raw collection of tiny habitations sitting in the lap of crouching hills. Above it hung a dim, bluish halo of woodsmoke, and Belle almost imagined that even from this distance she could hear the incessant whack of hammers and the buzz of handsaws.

"We'll have the picnic right over there," he told her eagerly, "under that tree. You can still get a fine view from there, yet it's out of the sun."

Looking at him impishly, she could not resist a crack. "You seem to know this place rather well, Ted."

The man was immediately flustered. "Of course," he told her. "I went looking for it as soon as you arrived in Sonora."

It was a gallant lie, and Belle was pleased to accept it for that. She could not expect a man such as Ted Manders would choose the life of a celibate while he waited for someone like her to arrive in Sonora. She hurried back to the surrey for the picnic basket and the blankets.

Belle had been careful not to prepare too much food and drink. She did not want their enjoyment dulled by the heaviness a full meal could cause. When the picnic was done and she had recovered the settings and put away the picnic basket, she returned to the blanket spread upon the pine needles and allowed him to take her in his arms. He had kissed her before, but this was a kiss meant for a beginning, not a polite good-bye—and she responded in kind.

It was perhaps unseemly, but they made love with a hungry intensity that astonished and gratified her. On fire from the moment his big hands first enclosed her, she could only urge him on, plead silently with him to complete what had become his promise to her.

And he kept it magnificently. He was all she had hoped he would be, his gentleness in no way preventing his surging power from taking her the way a woman craved. Afterward, she delighted him by proving that she could be all he might want in a woman as well, returning him to a potency and excitement that left him at last as satiated and gentle as a child.

The afternoon became a memory Belle would save for future unfolding.

Silent now, she sat with her back to a tree while Manders rested with his head on her lap. Both of them were fully dressed, but her hair, which reached almost to her waist, was not yet pinned back up, and Manders was playing with it idly.

"I have something to tell you," he said abruptly.

A knife-edge of panic slipped into her heart. Was he now going to tell her that he was married and that he must soon return east to his wife? "Go ahead," she managed, hoping that her voice did not betray the panic she suddenly felt.

He turned his head to look up at her face. "You said you wanted to know. It's about the mine."

Belle closed her eyes in relief. The mine and its troubles she could handle. A wife, she suddenly realized, was another matter entirely. Her earlier eagerness to broach the subject had vanished with the passion that had so recently consumed them.

"Go on then," she told him, brushing a lock of his hair off his forehead. "What about the mine?"

"It's just about played out, I'm afraid."

"Played out?"

"There is little gold left in the riverbed. And not a nugget in weeks. We have been sampling the riverbanks and the hills nearby. We've taken out just about all the gold there is, I'm afraid. We're down to washing the tailings."

"Then you'll leave to find another riverbed, won't you?"

He chuckled, reached up, and took her hand. "Yes, Belle. I guess that's just what I'll have to do. Find another riverbed."

She had no difficulty catching the amusement in his voice. "I gather that won't be easy."

"That's right. We won't see many more days like the one where an ox driver took twenty-six thousand dollars out of a single gulley." Manders shook his head in wonder. "It was not far from here . . . on the Stanislaus. Old John Sullivan is now building himself quite a bank in San Francisco, I hear. But that was early in the rush. Those boom days are gone. The little fellow with his wash pan and pack mule will soon be a thing of the past."

"You mean there's no more gold?"

"There's gold left, Belle. Plenty of it. But like my ex-partners have already found north of here, it takes engineering skills and heavy machinery to get it out. I told you how they were doing it—with water at high pressure. But have you any idea what it takes to divert the water in order to create such tremendous water pressure?"

"Not the faintest, Ted."

"Enormous labor and time, Belle. And great expense. Also a handy river nearby." Manders sighed. "Of course, there's another possibility—sinking shafts into the ground and removing the gold embedded in quartz veins with some kind of crushing equipment. I've seen a few miners lugging around crude stamp mills already. Like I said before, the days of the pick and shovel prospector are fast disappearing."

Belle did not want to ask the inevitable question, but she felt she had to do so. "How bad is it, Ted? Don't you have anything left?"

"I don't know." He smiled up at her then, somewhat wryly. "You suggested I go find another riverbed. . . ."

"I remember. You appeared to be somewhat amused."

"Amused isn't exactly the right word. You see, finding that other riverbed is the reason for my present dilemma."

"What do you mean?"

"I have sunk all the capital I have in a dig farther downstream from my present mine. This winter and spring I spent a fortune building the flume that diverted the stream. We've been digging in the emptied bed for weeks now, but so far we haven't found gold in anything like the quantities I had counted on. We haven't given up, though. Our luck could change."

"But it doesn't look good."

He sighed. "I must be honest with you, Belle. No, it doesn't."

"And if the gold you expected is not there, then all this money you spent to divert the stream is lost."

"Yes. It was an investment, Belle—and not all investments pan out."

Belle took a deep breath. "I see."

"It looks like you've been dallying with a used-up man,"

Manders said, his voice somber, "a perfect used-up man, as the song goes. Too bad."

"Hush," she told him sharply. "Don't talk like that."

She bent then and kissed him lightly on the forehead. In that instant Belle knew she had fallen in love with Ted Manders. She had come all this way to find a man who had the gumption to strike it rich and then hold on to it. Ted Manders did not exactly meet that requirement, and that should have made a difference.

But it didn't.

After leaving O'Hare to finish off the dying Prentiss, Rafe rode back to the spot where they had first encountered the wounded man and his companion. Recalling the Cortland woman's account of her struggle with Coleman, he moved up the hillside just above where the wagon had sat, and searched the ground for any tracks left by Coleman or any sign of blood.

Almost at once Rafe picked up Coleman's trail. The man, digging frantically in the soft ground with his heavy boots, had charged off into the timber. Though it was next to impossible to track a man on a floor of pine needles, Rafe was not deterred. Leading his horse behind him, Rafe saw where the panic-stricken Coleman had crashed through brambles, snapped dry branches that lay across his path—and in general had done all he could to leave a trail someone could follow. Soon, Rafe noticed drops of blood on rocks and on the leaves of bushes and saplings in his path.

It was midafternoon when he came upon Coleman.

Stepping out of the timber, he caught sight of the wounded merchant less than twenty yards from him, crouched under a pine. Coleman could go no farther, it appeared. Beyond him the ground dropped away into a deep chasm. On the far side, at least a mile distant, a wall of tiered rock climbed at least another hundred feet. From where Rafe stood, the towering pines on its brink looked like toy trees.

Coleman turned at Rafe's approach. He was in a state

bordering on panic, and his first reaction upon seeing Rafe was alarm. Rafe smiled. At once Coleman called out to him.

"I'm wounded!" he cried. "Help me!"

Dropping his horse's reins, Rafe walked toward Coleman. "How bad are you hurt?"

"It's my side. I've been shot in the side!"

"Who did this to you, amigo?" Rafe inquired pleasantly as he halted beside the man.

"Never mind that!" snapped Coleman.

Rafe smiled again. The gringo did not want it known that he had been wounded by a woman he had tried to rape. "Show me where you are hurt," Rafe said. "I will see if I can help."

Like a sick dog, Coleman rolled over on the grass, exposing a bloody stain in his shirt with a small hole in its center where the round had entered. Ignoring Coleman's yelp of protest, Rafe tore the shirt brutally away from the site of the hole and examined the wound carefully. It was a superficial but undoubtedly painful flesh wound. Had the man not panicked and run off as he had, chances are he could easily have stopped the bleeding simply by binding it securely.

Without a word, Rafe stood up and returned to his horse. Leading it over to a sapling, he tied it up and, ignoring Coleman, walked past the man to the edge of the clearing. Then he looked down into the chasm, where a river wound through the gorge at least three hundred yards below. It was a tributary of the Stanislaus, Rafe was pretty certain, and flowed into Johnson Creek, another stream, which gave Sonora most of its water.

From the many white patches on its surface, Rafe knew it was a swift-running, tumultuous river with a roar that could be heard for miles. At each bend in its channel, he could see faint, mistlike clouds of spray hanging above it. Yet from this height Rafe could hear nothing.

He turned and went back to Coleman.

"You'll have to help me back through the timber," Coleman told him in a whining, arrogant voice.

"You think so?" Rafe smiled.

"Of course!" It was obvious Coleman was aware that Rafe was Mexican. "You better let me ride your horse," the store owner told him. "It would be easier for me that way."

"Tell me, Coleman," Rafe asked gently. "Who shot you?"

"You know my name?"

"Yes, I know your name. So now, maybe you tell me. Who shot you? And then maybe you tell me why."

Panic flared in Coleman's face. He was a rabbit cornered.

Rafe smiled. "Was it maybe a woman who shot you?"

"It was a mistake!" Coleman bleated. "She misunderstood! And then I had to fight off that clerk of mine. He did it! It was he who was after her! I am innocent!"

"Perhaps so," Rafe said, reasonably. "And were you also innocent of the death of Josita Escobar?"

The man was plainly confused. "Josita Escobar?"

"Yes. My wife. It happened two years ago. But that was such a long time ago. You have maybe forgotten."

"Forgotten? I . . . look, I don't understand."

Leaning forward, Rafe slapped Coleman on the side of his face, hard. "Perhaps that will help you to remember. It was your wagon Josita stood on. It was you who cracked the whip!"

For one more moment Coleman looked up at Rafe, utterly confused. Then came comprehension—sudden and devastating. He groaned.

"Ah, you do remember. It was a long time ago. And she was just a Mexican whore. But you remember. Is that not so?"

"Oh, God! And you . . . you're her husband?"

"Her widower. And now I am your executioner."

"You're mad! You can't do this. There was a trial! Your wife was convicted of murdering a man!"

"Gringo justice!" Rafe spat.

Lifting his revolver from his belt, he aimed it down at Coleman. With a shriek of terror, Coleman began to crawl along the ground away from Rafe, a loathesome, mewling worm that excited in Rafe only disgust. That such a piece of offal should have taken part in the death of his wife was insupportable.

Indeed as if he were herding some loathesome worm, Rafe headed Coleman off and turned him so that he was moving at last toward the edge of the clearing. It did not take long for Coleman to perceive Rafe's intent. He glanced behind him at the gorge yawning at his back, then sprang to his feet, terror banishing all thought of his superficial wound.

"You can't do this!" he cried. "It's murder! Cold-blooded murder!"

"You murdered Josita. You and the rest of that mob!"

In a frenzy of fear, Coleman dropped to his knees. Raising clasped hands, he pleaded for his life. "I was caught up in it. I did not want to bring my wagon up that night. For the love of God, have mercy!"

Rafe frowned. Even he could not kill a man *this* craven—no matter what the reason. The devil himself would roast him if he did.

"Show courage, you ball of slime," Rafe told Coleman, stepping back. "Rush me! . . . Look!" Rafe broke open his revolver and spun the cylinders, allowing the cartridges to drop to the ground. "You see? I am unarmed!"

Coleman hesitated. He could not believe what he had just seen.

"Do you want to die?" Rafe asked reasonably. "If not, then fight! Show courage, in the name of God."

With a frenzied cry born of desperation, Coleman charged Rafe. Waiting calmly, the smaller man sidestepped Coleman neatly and brought the barrel of his six-gun down on the back of Coleman's neck. The fellow sagged to his knees, pawing at the ground like a blind man.

Rafe stepped back and waited.

Somehow Coleman managed to get back up. With an inarticulate cry, he plunged blindly at Rafe, tears of rage streaming down his face. For a moment the two grappled.

Then completely out of patience with the man's hysterical sniveling, Rafe again clubbed Coleman to the ground.

Dazed, weeping like a child, Coleman sat up on his haunches, cowering before Rafe. He was too beaten to get up a second time. At last, his patience at an end and feeling only loathing for the whimpering excuse for a man groveling before him, Rafe grabbed Coleman under his chin and dragged him to the edge of the clearing. Coleman screamed. Taking a deep breath, Rafe swung Coleman out over the rim and let go. Still screaming, Coleman vanished.

Stepping closer to the edge, Rafe looked down and caught sight of Coleman's body as it struck a jutting finger of rock and flew loosely outward. A moment later, still twisting slowly, Coleman vanished into the silent ribbon of water.

There was no exultation within Rafe as he turned away and started across the clearing toward his horse, just a dull weariness. A moment later, he mounted up and vanished into the timber.

O'Hare's compassion had again caused him to do the unexpected.

Telling himself that he was unwilling to lug a bleeding corpse all the way up to the burial site, where José already lay buried, he had slung the feverish Prentiss over his shoulder and started up the path toward the clearing. Killing Prentiss on the spot where he intended to bury him would be a lot neater, he rationalized.

When he reached the gravesite, he eased the man down onto the grass. Removing his hat, O'Hare wiped his brow with the back of his forearm, then peered wearily down at the valley.

A pretty enough hideaway, he decided, but it sure as hell didn't feel too peaceful to him. It was turning into a graveyard—Rafe's graveyard. And Brett O'Hare was becoming its chief gravedigger. The thought caused him to stir uncomfortably, and he glanced down at Prentiss, whose face had a flushed, hectic glow from the fever. His breathing was coming in short, shallow gasps. But the man was alive—indubitably alive—despite his loss of blood.

O'Hare looked back at the cabin, now a small toy far below, and then he gazed in the opposite direction up the slope. A large boulder caught his attention, and after staring at it for a full minute, he realized that he wanted to find a way to avoid killing Dan Prentiss. He had not shot Prentiss earlier because . . . *he had simply not wanted to kill the man*.

Just as he had chosen not to kill that fool miner.

And just as he had not wanted to kill Ellen.

Turning with sudden decision toward Prentiss, O'Hare grabbed the man's shoulder and shook him, hard.

"Hey!" he called. "Prentiss!"

The man's heavy eyelids moved slightly. Again, O'Hare shook him. Prentiss opened his eyes and stared dimly at O'Hare.

Satisfied, O'Hare swung Prentiss up onto his shoulder, paused only a moment to gain his balance, then carried him up to the boulder and moved in behind it. He was right—there was plenty of space behind it to hide a body. Easing himself around the huge rock, O'Hare was astonished to find what appeared to be a mine opening still farther in. No matter. He had other business at the moment.

Gently setting Prentiss down, he shook the unconscious man violently until he opened his eyes once again.

"Listen to me," O'Hare commanded. "You don't know me, but that don't matter. Do you want to live?"

Frowning in confusion, Prentiss stared fuzzily at O'Hare.

"*Do* you, dammit?"

Prentiss managed a nod.

"Good! Now listen. Stay here tonight. Maybe you will live and maybe you won't. But whatever happens don't return to Sonora. If you do, you'll be a dead man. Is that clear?"

"Dead . . . man . . ." Prentiss repeated dully.

"Yes. A dead man. Stay in here until tomorrow. I

don't care where the hell you go after that, but don't go back to Sonora. Or I won't be able to help you."

O'Hare examined Prentiss's bandages then. They were beginning to smell bad, he noticed. Resting a palm on the wounded man's forehead, he pulled it back with a grunt. The poor sonofabitch was on fire. It would be a miracle if he lasted through the night.

Feeling only slightly better about things, O'Hare backed out from behind the boulder and hurried down the slope for a shovel.

He was sitting cross-legged beside a fresh mound of earth next to José's grave when Rafe rode back into the valley a little before sundown. O'Hare took the cigar he was smoking out of his mouth and jumped up, waving down to Rafe. When Rafe climbed up to the burial site and saw O'Hare standing beside the fresh grave, a shovel in his hand, he nodded wearily, satisfied.

"We go back now to Sonora," he muttered to O'Hare.

O'Hare offered no objection. He was only too willing to leave this corpse-ridden valley of Rafe's and get back to the Gold Nugget's gaming tables. He could draw to an inside straight, perhaps. But he could not, it seemed, kill a man.

Not in cold blood.

Chapter 8

Sharon was prepared to see some raised eyebrows when she rode into the mining camp. What she had not been prepared for was the sudden, almost palpable silence that fell over the men as they caught sight of her. To her astonishment and dismay, all work stopped. As she pulled the team to a halt and climbed down, miners singly and in groups appeared as if from nowhere and gathered around the freight wagon to stare dumbly at her. The hush deepened when she stood at last on the ground beside the wagon, flung her long hair back over her shoulders, and turned to face what resembled an awe-struck multitude. She cleared her throat nervously.

"Mr. Coleman . . . is not with me," she said, her voice ringing out over the massed men with a startling, bell-like clarity. "And if you please, I would like someone to help me unload the wagon."

At first there was no movement. The men continued to gaze upon her. Then, abruptly, their ranks broke, and the miners swept past her, climbing up onto the wagon like monkeys after a harvest of bananas. Then the unsettling silence was broken by encouraging shouts from the men.

"No need to worry, ma'am! We'll have this wagon unloaded in no time!"

"Just leave it to us!"

"You just stand aside. We know where this goes!"

"Someone fetch Alexander!"

"Here he comes!"

From her conversations with Coleman on the trip from Sonora, Sharon knew that Mr. Alexander was his junior partner who ran the supply store in the mining camp. As he emerged from the swarm of miners, she was startled to see he was a bowed ancient with a long white beard.

With barely a glance at her and with a spryness that belied his skeletal appearance, he dug out the precious mail sacks first and then took charge of the unloading. At once the miners began hauling down the barrels and trunks, which they lugged toward a large, log building located on high ground above the miner's ramshackle living quarters. Leading the way, Alexander unlocked the door and flung it open.

Back alongside the freight wagon, the other men had gathered around a miner with steel-rimmed spectacles and a tattered, muddy frock coat. Standing on a tree stump, he was digging into one of the mail sacks and calling out names.

Watching the miners crowd around the fellow in the frock coat, Sharon was struck by the joy those who rushed off clutching their letters exhibited—and the tragic hope and anxiety etched so vividly on the faces of those still waiting for their names to be called. Soon—all too soon for those still standing there—the tattered gentleman in the spectacles held up the two empty mail sacks for all to see, then stepped down from the stump. The unhappy miners still clustered around him looked with desolate eyes at their companions—then turned and went their separate ways, despair and loneliness marking each face.

Turning back to the store, Sharon entered and found a long line of men waiting to purchase the necessities, while other miners continued to load provisions onto the sagging shelves. She was reluctant to approach any of the miners, so disconcerted were they in her presence.

So long had these men been without women that they looked at Sharon as if they were gazing on a creature just dropped from the moon. It made Sharon distinctly uneasy, especially when she caught some glances that were not altogether innocent—that in fact sent shivers down her spine. At such moments the horror of her nighttime encounter with Coleman swept over her, and her knees turned to water.

Still, she had come to find her brother. And find him she would. She had hoped to hear his voice call out to her from the crowd that had gathered, silent and awed, when she pulled the wagon to a halt. That she had not heard him did not discourage her, however. He might be at the diggings on the hill, after all.

This was the hope she clung to as she finally mustered up her courage and slipped behind the counter, where Mr. Alexander was busy weighing out the miner's piles of gold so they could make purchases. As she waited for a chance to speak to the old man, she did her best to keep out of his way as he moved from side to side, hunched over his beard and not once looking up at the young woman. She intended to ask him for permission to question the miners as they purchased their goods. Surely there was a chance one of them might know of Tim's whereabouts. The old man appeared so busy, though, that she was reluctant to disturb him.

Her appearance behind the counter had hushed up the men, though it did not quiet them completely. More than a few furtive glances were flung her way, which she did her best to ignore. Mr. Alexander finally left off dealing with one of his customers, and pushing his scales to one side, he turned to her.

"Do you have to stand here, ma'am?" he asked, his voice soft but firm. "You're making the men nervous. Why don't you go in the back room and rest up. I won't be finished here before dark, I'm thinking."

"Let her be!" someone in the back shouted. "She looks just fine standing there!"

"Prettiest thing in the place!" another called.

"Ask Coleman how much he wants for her!"

This crack brought angry rejoinders from those standing near the unfortunate who made it. Sharon saw the fellow visibly wilt and almost felt sorry for him.

Seizing the opportunity, Sharon spoke out. "I am looking for my brother, Tim Cortland. I have come all the way from Maine to find him. Do any of you know him? Has any of you seen him?"

The men grew still as everyone, like Sharon, waited for a voice to reply. Miners turned to look around them, hoping to see someone respond. But no one did.

A note of desperation creeping into her voice, Sharon went on. "He has a friend who Mr. Coleman said was still up here. His name is Peter Wilder. Does anyone here know him? Peter Wilder?"

"Sure!" cried a fellow in back. "I know Pete. He's on the other side of Pine Hill. He won't be back until tonight."

Smiling suddenly, Sharon took a deep breath. A few of the miners broke into grins as they looked back at her, and Sharon saw the reflection of her joy on the face of each man watching her.

"Thank you," she said, addressing the miner who had just spoken. "If you or anyone else sees Pete before I do, would you please tell him that Tim Cortland's sister is here?"

"Ma'am," the fellow replied, his bearded face breaking into a broad grin, "this whole camp knows about you by now. Word gets around pretty fast in these diggings. You just stay put. Pete will find you."

Booming laughter erupted in the room. The men seemed suddenly as relaxed and pleased as Sharon. Blushing at their warmth, she thanked the men, then took Mr. Alexander's advice and pushed her way through the door that led into the back room.

A single dirt-encrusted window provided only dim light, but she was able to catch sight of a single cot against the far wall, a wood stove in the center, and a table and chairs close by the window. Slumping into one of the chairs, she crossed her arms on the table and lay her head down on them.

Then, to her own surprise, she began to cry—softly, silently.

Even as she cried, she realized she was simply giving vent to the tension kept bottled within her since the day she first set out for California. Now she could afford the luxury of tears. What she was attempting no longer seemed such an impossible task. She was really getting close! Nearby was a friend of her brother's, and soon he would come and tell her where Tim was!

Lifting her head at last, she brushed away her tears and yawned, which reminded her of how exhausted she had been during the ride to the diggings. She got to her feet and just managed to make it to the cot—collapsing face down on it—before she fell into a deep, dreamless sleep.

Someone was bending over her. She awoke with a start and sat up, momentarily disoriented, wondering if she were reliving her struggle with Jim Coleman in a nightmare. It was almost completely dark in the room, the only illumination coming from the moonlight filtering through the window.

"Who . . . who is it?" she managed.

The figure straightened and retreated to the table. A moment later she saw Mr. Alexander light a candle and bring it and a chair over to the cot. Setting the candle down on the floor, he placed the chair alongside the cot and sat down.

"The freight wagon will be ready to leave for Sonora first thing in the morning," he told her. "The horses will be fresh enough by then. You will have much gold to take back, and that worries me. What about Jim Coleman? He didn't send you out here alone, did he?"

Sitting up in the bed, she leaned her back against the wall. "He made the trip with me, Mr. Alexander."

"Then where is he?"

"I don't know."

"Miss, I don't understand you. If he made the trip, where is he?"

"Your partner—Mr. Jim Coleman—attacked me. If it were not for an acquaintance of mine who followed us, Jim Coleman would have . . ." She did not have to finish the sentence. One look at Mr. Alexander's face and she knew he understood perfectly.

Grimly, Mr. Alexander nodded. "I am sorry to hear Jim attacked you. Now please go on. What happened after that?"

"We struggled for his gun, and it went off. He was shot. If I could have, I would have killed him. But he ran off."

"Then you did not kill him."

"A man running that fast could not possibly be near death. But I had a gun and I was attempting to shoot him. I wanted very much to kill him."

Mr. Alexander leaned back and gazed at her, the slightest trace of a smile on his pinched face. "You pretty near frightened Jim Coleman to death, I'm thinking."

"I really don't care. Mr. Coleman seriously wounded my friend, a Mr. Dan Prentiss. I was forced to leave Dan with two other men, since I was unable to care for him myself. And I wanted to reach here as soon as possible."

Mr. Alexander nodded solemnly, then took a deep breath. "What you are saying, ma'am, is that my partner, Jim Coleman, tried to rape you and may be responsible for the death of the man who came to your aid."

"Yes," she snapped. "That is it exactly."

"Would you have any objections if I did not keep this a secret? I think the miners in this camp should know what Jim Coleman attempted—just in case he should show up here."

It only took a few seconds for Sharon to make up her mind. "No," she said decisively. "I would not mind at all."

Mr. Alexander nodded. "Under the circumstances,

ma'am, I guess I'd better be the one who takes that freight wagon back. And the gold."

"Mr. Alexander, all I want is to find my brother, Tim."

"I understand that." He got up from the chair, took a blanket from the bottom of the bed, and drew it up around Sharon's shoulders. "I'll sleep in one of the miner's tents. There's more than one out there who owe me. You get your sleep now."

He picked up the candle, blew it out, and left the room.

It was near dawn when Sharon was awakened once again—this time by someone outside rapping on the glass. Throwing back her blanket, she ran to the window and peered through the dirty pane. A young man's face was pressing against it.

The close proximity of the man made Sharon gasp. She then swallowed hard and asked, "Who are you?"

"Pete Wilder! I've come to take you to your brother!"

Sharon could hardly believe her ears. With a tiny shriek, she grabbed the window sash and after a brief struggle managed to raise it enough for Pete Wilder to climb in.

"But why didn't you come earlier?" Sharon asked.

Wilder grinned. "I owe Coleman a small fortune, that's why. I try to keep my distance from him and Alexander. Come on. We can leave now. I took your gear from the wagon. There's two horses out back."

"But where's Tim?"

"At a place we ain't told nobody about. Our pans been showing shine for a week now. Not much, but the strike might get bigger. A whole lot bigger!"

"How did you hear about me?"

He took her by the shoulder and brought her gently over to the open window so that the moonlight shone directly on her face. "That's how. There's no way a flower pretty as you can be kept a secret in these hills. Now, let's go. I want to clear out of this place 'fore sunup."

A sudden, terrifying suspicion leaped into her mind. How could she be sure this was indeed Tim's friend?

"But why didn't Tim come himself?"

"You know him! He's off on a wild goose chase in the hills north of our camp. That boy ain't never satisfied with panning for gold. He wants to find nuggets. Says he wants to keep a promise he made to you."

Sharon held her breath. "And what was that?"

"To bring you a necklace of gold nuggets so you could buy yourself a real piano."

Sharon breathed a deep sigh of relief. Only from Tim could Pete have learned about that promise made to her on the dockside the day he boarded ship for Panama.

"Let's hurry," she cried.

"You first," Pete said, boosting Sharon out through the window.

After somewhat of a delay, Pete followed her out the window. He was carrying a duffel bag laden with goods. Evidently, he had been pilfering the store's shelves.

"That's not very nice," Sharon said, as the two hurried across a moonlit clearing toward the waiting horses.

Pete chuckled. "Might as well owe for a bushel as a pound."

A moment later, they were riding out of camp, a packhorse trailing them. Beating the sun by no more than minutes, they disappeared into the timber.

Chapter 9

T he same rising sun that hastened Sharon and Pete Wilder into the timber that morning awoke Dan Prentiss. The sun stamped a small corner of the ground behind the boulder with a clarion brightness that caused Dan to blink uncomfortably and turn his face away. When he tried to raise his head a moment later, a solid wall of rock gave it a nasty crack. Reaching up to feel his head, his hand also struck the encroaching wall.

My God, he thought. *Where the hell am I?*

For a terrible, unnerving moment Dan wondered if he might have been buried alive. Tales of such horror had always fascinated him. But turning his head cautiously, he saw once again the pristine shaft of light slanting into the darkness and knew at once that his tomb could not be airless. With a weary groan of relief, he began pulling himself out from the wall.

His thigh—no, his entire right side!—burned with sudden stabs of pain. Gritting his teeth against it, he sat up and rested his back on a slope behind. As he looked carefully about his prison, he found himself staring at the side of what appeared to be an enormous boulder. He reached out to touch its cool surface just to make sure, and the sunlight increased its glow, brightening his dank shelter.

Cautiously, Dan again looked around him. In the glow of the sun's reflected light, he glimpsed what appeared to be the opening to a mine shaft about nine or ten feet to his left. *These damned hills must be alive with abandoned mines*, he told himself as he looked once again toward the sunlight. He was anxious to flee his tomb and was determined to do so—no matter what agony the movement would cause him. Despite the raw pain that immediately erupted in his thigh, he dragged himself the rest of the way out from behind the boulder.

As soon as he was in the open and his eyes became accustomed to the sudden brightness, he examined his wound. Someone—Sharon perhaps—had torn up his shirt and wrapped the strips around his thigh. But over the wound the bandages had become a blood-hardened carapace. And from under that shell came a smell so rank it made his stomach shift queasily.

He decided to take off the bandage. Reaching down awkwardly, he grabbed it. The moment his fingers closed about the bloody shield, however, a sharp, sickening stab of pain rocketed from the thigh, clear up into his torso. So great was the pain that as he pulled his hand away, tears sprang into his eyes. It was as if the teeth of some fiendish animal were fastened to his thigh. And if he were going to survive, he would have to slice it out—teeth, thigh, and all—without mercy.

He leaned back in an effort to gain control. Gradually the pain in his thigh eased somewhat. He took a deep breath and closed his eyes. The next moment he found himself recalling dimly the words of someone looming close to him. He was being warned, something about not going back to Sonora. But that made no sense. None at all.

Oh, hell, nothing made sense. Why in blazes had he been stuffed behind that boulder? And where were Sharon and that sonofabitch, Coleman? But the more questions he asked, the more confused he got. The only thing that really mattered was this gnawing pain in his right thigh

. . . and that even though he was lying out here in the bright morning sunshine of midsummer, he was shivering as if it were the middle of winter!

He was hurt bad. And he was alone. *The only one who could save him was himself.* At once, this exasperated admonition seemed to help. He felt less woozy, less out of contact with the world. Squinting around him in the bright sunlight, he discovered he was high on a slope. Below him lay a small, lush valley, a bright stream slicing through the middle of it. At the far end, he glimpsed a small cabin.

His best bet would be to make for that cabin, he realized. Whoever lived there might be skilled enough with gunshot wounds to help him. At least there would be water; his mouth was as dry as an old newspaper. The trouble was, could he drag himself that far? Well, he wouldn't know if he didn't try.

Ignoring the pain in his thigh, he leaned over and proceeded to pull himself along through the grass, inching toward the distant cabin below him like a great, wounded snake.

Sharon was angry. And disappointed. Though Pete Wilder was putting up a good show, there was no longer any doubt in Sharon's mind that he was not telling her the truth.

They had just finished their noon meal at Wilder's camp. Sharon had prepared it, using the provisions Wilder had pilfered from the store back at the Pine Hill diggings. The camp was no more than a patched canvas tent with an outside campfire, a miserable hole behind a nearby clump of pine serving as a privy. There was a stream, but not the slightest indication that any panning or digging for gold had been going on anywhere in the vicinity. And though Wilder had talked about other miners waiting to greet them, it was clear that this, too, was a lie.

This was a solitary camp. Wilder was alone—completely alone. And there was no sign at all of Tim or any of his gear.

"Hadn't you better tell me the truth, Peter?" Sharon said abruptly.

Wilder had been in the act of lugging his gear into the tent when Sharon spoke. He stopped in his tracks.

"What do you mean, Sharon?"

"There are no other miners here."

"Must have cleared out. Miners are like that. The way they look at it, there's always better paydirt over the next hill."

"I don't see any sign at all that you or anyone else has been mining this creek. None at all."

He smiled disarmingly. "I told you, Sharon. We want to keep it quiet. All our tools are hid, and we're filling up any holes we dig. It's just a precaution."

"Show me where you have hidden your tools."

"Aw, Sharon, honey, take my word for it."

"Why should I? I never met you before this morning. You seem pleasant enough, but I think you are irresponsible. You stole these provisions from Mr. Alexander. And now I am certain you are a liar."

"But Tim and me were friends."

Sharon held her breath. "*Were?* Did you say *were* friends?"

Wilder caught himself. Flustered, he looked suddenly away from Sharon. "Damn," he said. "I was going to say something. I just been stalling 'cause I didn't know how to tell you."

Sharon forced herself to take a deep breath. "Tell me," she heard herself say. "And tell me right now. Do you mean you and Tim are no longer friends? Or . . . has something happened to Tim?"

Wilder looked squarely at Sharon. "I reckon it's worse than that. I'm sorry, Sharon. But Tim's dead."

Sharon gasped. "No!" she cried. "I don't believe you!"

"I guess I can understand that. I ain't been very square with you. But it's the truth, the God's truth, Sharon. I wouldn't say such a thing if it weren't true."

Sharon had gone numb all over. Sagging to the ground, she stared blankly ahead with her mouth open, emitting

spasmodic groans of agony. This was not happening. . . .
Tim had to be alive. *Wilder must be lying*, she thought.
Her head was shaking in negation as she moaned, "No
. . . no . . ." again and again. Then she began to sob
brokenly, raggedly. Wilder rushed to her side, trying to
comfort her, but she thrust him away, furious.

She felt as if a violent storm were passing through
her, tearing down all the structure to her life. Losing all
track of time, she was only dimly aware of coiling herself
into a ball and crying out as Wilder attempted over and
over to calm her. At last he pulled back and left her,
seemingly as distraught as she. He had never seen a
woman this taken with grief.

Only gradually did the storm within Sharon let up.
The uncontrollable sobbing gave way to a dry, choking
cough. Drying her eyes at last, she was surprised at how
raw and sore they felt. She felt her face; her cheeks were
puffy. Suddenly she became aware that her hair was hanging shroudlike over her eyes.

Glancing up, she saw Wilder. He was some distance
from her, hunkered down beside the campfire, watching
her carefully—in the cautious, fearful way one would watch
something wild and ungovernable.

Pushing her hair wearily back over her shoulder, she
told him faintly that she was all right now. As she spoke, a
dry sob, like a hiccup, came out unbidden.

Wilder got to his feet and approached her, still wary.

Sharon looked up at him. "Tell me," she said. "Was it
the cholera that killed him?"

He sat down carefully on the grass before her. "No. It
wasn't the cholera."

"Tell me then. What was it?"

"Tim and Amos Wheeler, a partner of ours, got themselves killed."

Sharon closed her eyes for an instant. Why was the truth
always so much worse than you imagined? She opened her
eyes. "How, Peter? How did such a thing happen?"

"It's kind of complicated, Sharon."

"I don't care how complicated it is. Tell me. I want to know."

"All right. I'll tell you what I know for sure."

Pete explained that Tim and Amos had stumbled upon a cabin hidden away in a valley somewhere south of Pine Hill. Prospecting at the time, they had ducked inside it to get out of a downpour. Once inside, they discovered gold dust on the floors and all over the makeshift furniture. Sweeping most of it up, they managed to gather enough to fill a couple of deerskin pouches, which they had gleefully pocketed.

"You mean . . . Tim *stole* the gold dust?" Sharon's voice sounded unsteady again.

"Now, I wouldn't rightly say that. Tim wasn't keen on out-an' out thievery. Amos was the one, I reckon. Anyway, they figured there must be a lode nearby, so the two of them settled in to wait. They were going to convince the owner, you see, to lead them to his mine."

"You mean, force the man to take them to his mine?" Sharon asked.

Wilder nodded.

"Go on," Sharon said grimly.

Tim and Amos had waited several days without any luck, Pete said. "They were running out of food and getting just plain edgy, so Tim came into town—that's when I saw him."

"But he went back—"

"Yes, ma'am. I helped him load up with bacon and buckshot and other things. Then Tim and me came here. We made up this camp, and then Tim went back to the cabin to wait for the owner. I never saw Tim or Amos alive again. Some miners found their bodies near the road to Sonora, each one with a bullet hole in the back. Near as I can figure it," Pete added, finishing up his account, "the owner of that cabin was a damn sight tougher to deal with than either Tim or Amos counted on."

"Where was this cabin?" Sharon asked.

Wilder shrugged. "All I know is Tim mentioned a split pine sitting atop a ledge at the entrance to the valley where the cabin was. I been searching for it myself for the past couple of months, but I can't find it. There must be a hundred valleys in this here mountain range. I ain't never seen the like."

Sharon held her breath, then looked quickly away from Wilder. Not only did she know where that cabin was, but she also realized that her brother's murderer was very possibly one of the two men who had taken Dan Prentiss with them into that valley.

"Is there something wrong?" Wilder asked, frowning suddenly. He then reached over and put his arms around Sharon.

With an angry cry, Sharon twisted around, attempting to pull free of Wilder, but he would not let her go. He clung to her desperately from behind.

"Please, Sharon!" he cried as he struggled to restrain her. "I just want to take care of you. I was Tim's friend."

Furious, Sharon dug her fingernails between the bones of the hands that held her. When Wilder, grimacing, relaxed his grip, Sharon was ready. She pried back his fingers, jumped to her feet, and raced to the packhorse. Ripping open a saddlebag, she pulled out the same enormous revolver Coleman had used on Dan Prentiss, the weapon that she had had the presence of mind to retrieve from the ground where she had dropped it.

Swinging around, she brought up the revolver. Less than five yards from her, Wilder scrambled to a halt, his eyes wide. She aimed the gun at his chest, using both hands to steady it.

"No, Sharon!" he cried. "Please!"

"So this is how Tim's friend treats his sister." She spat the words out scornfully. "Some friend!"

"Don't shoot!"

Sharon glared at him, too angry to speak.

"Please?" Wilder's chest now heaved in terror.

"Turn around!"

Wilder spun, then scrunched his shoulders, waiting for the shot. He was shaking all over. Walking up behind him, Sharon lifted the heavy revolver over her head, her fist around the barrel, then paused. She could not get herself to bring it down on Wilder's head. It was too fearful a thing to do to another human being—even one as repulsive as Pete Wilder.

"Get down on your hands and knees," she ordered.

Promptly, Wilder did as he was bid.

"Stay like that and don't move!"

"What are you going to do?" Wilder bleated.

"You'll find out soon enough."

Keeping a sharp eye on him, she hurried back to Wilder's horse and lifted the leather reata, which was looped around the saddle horn. Then she hurried back to Wilder and swiftly wound the reata around his ankles. Unceremoniously yanking his arms behind his back, she secured the trembling man's wrists in the same fashion, and then bound wrists and ankles together.

Standing back to view her handiwork, she was satisfied. Sprawled on his side, Wilder looked like a trussed turkey. All he could do was flop about on his stomach.

"You can't leave me like this!" he cried. "There's bears in this country. And wolves!"

"I know that," Sharon said soberly. "I just want time to get far away from you. Look over at that stand of pine. How far would you say that is from here?"

He twisted his head around and ventured a guess. "Three hundred, maybe four hundred yards."

"Where's that hunting knife you had?"

"On my cot inside the tent. But you can't—"

"I'll leave it behind that foremost pine. It'll take you a while to get that far. But when you do, you can cut yourself loose."

"My God! I'll never make it!"

"Yes, you will. Remember those bears . . . and the wolves."

She took his hunting knife from the tent, ran over with it to the pine, and dropped it where she had promised she would. Then she gathered up all of his cooking gear and anything else he might be able to use to cut through his bonds and dropped them behind another pine deeper into the timber. Twisting his head around, he watched her balefully, but said nothing.

Certain it would be some time before Wilder managed to free himself, she bid him a curt good-bye and strode over to her horse. After replacing the revolver and checking to see that she had all her other gear, she hoisted herself up. Adjusting her skirt, she made herself as comfortable as she could be on the western saddle, then struck the horse's flanks with her heels and set off.

She knew where she was going. During her ride from the Pine Hill diggings with Wilder, she had kept careful note of her bearings. The roadway she had taken from Sonora to get to Pine Hill was due south, she figured. Once she gained that road, she could continue south on it toward Sonora.

Then as soon as she caught sight of that long meadow below the trail and the single white pine atop the ridge beyond it, she would know where to go from there.

It was close to sunset by the time Dan Prentiss reached the cabin. Somehow he managed to reach up and push the door open and crawl inside. For the last quarter of an hour or so he had been calling out in desperate hope that he would arouse whoever might be inside. But the closer he got, the more desolate the place appeared to him, and at the last he had given up on the possibility.

Now sprawled on the floor, he looked around at the deserted cabin's interior. All it could offer him was shelter. For now, that was enough.

Along one wall was an army cot, and above it ran shelves with dusty cans of food. Two windows let in enough of the fading light to reveal a wood stove in the corner. A deal table and two chairs completed the meager furnishings.

He crawled to the cot and pulled himself onto it. Carefully, he sat up. He felt unnaturally warm. For the last hour or so he had been sweating profusely, though the sun was hovering close to the horizon and a cooling breeze had sprung up. He was aware, also, that he was having difficulty keeping a rein on his thoughts. They seemed disordered, out of control, even crazy at times. He could not be sure, but he had the impression that once he had reached the valley floor that afternoon, he had passed out. Yet he couldn't be sure—of that or of anything else.

He looked down at the bandage still wrapped around his thigh. During his long painful crawl to the cabin, portions had fallen off, and now all that was left was a crusted section that formed a scab over the wound itself. Feeling reckless and half wild with despair, Dan reached down and, without forethought, ripped the hardened bandage off the wound.

It was like unstoppering a foul sink. Black ooze swelled from the wound as a searing pain swept up the length of his thigh. He found himself panting from the awful, all-consuming pain. Carefully, he eased himself back on the cot, trying not to mind the stench of his corruption.

At that moment he heard a sound outside the door. As he turned his head toward it, the door swung open to reveal Sharon Cortland standing hesitantly in the doorway. She did not seem to see him at first in the dim light, but then her eyes picked him out on the cot. With a cry, she rushed toward him.

But he did not want her this close! He tried to push her away. She must not see him like this! He could not bear to have her smell the awful infestation welling out of his thigh.

She pushed him down gently, insistently, then picked up a candle and searched the cabin for a match. A moment later, when she looked down at his wound, she uttered a cry and almost dropped her lit candle.

"Oh, Dan," she said, "it must hurt so!"

He managed a smile and suddenly felt a hundred percent better. "It does at that—when my head stops spinning, that is."

Swiftly reaching over, she pressed a cool hand to his brow. "And you have such a fever!"

"I think if I could just clean out this wound . . ."

"Of course. That's what we'll do first."

He leaned back, listening as she rummaged in a cabinet alongside the stove and pulled out a deep tin pan. She vanished out the door and returned in a few minutes with the pan filled with water from the stream. It was not long before she had the wood stove glowing, the pan of water steaming.

Then she ripped one of her slips into squares and dropped them into the boiling water. Not long after, she told him she was going to scrub his wound clean and that he should put something in his mouth to bite down on— the way a woman might do when she was giving birth— when she began the operation.

"Only this, I am afraid, is going to be much more painful than childbirth," she told him. "I really do need to scrub it out to get rid of all that dead flesh."

"I don't care. Do it."

She handed him a tough piece of leather. It looked like a scrap of old harness. "Bite down on this. I found it near the door outside and cleaned it off in the stream."

He took the leather from her, placing it carefully in his mouth and biting down on it. Grimly, he nodded to her to proceed.

Turning back to the stove, she lifted out a boiling piece of her cotton slip with a stick, waited for it to cool sufficiently, then wrung it out. He could see how much it stung her to handle the steaming cloth. She approached him, and Dan turned away and clamped his jaw down hard on the leather.

There were tears in Sharon's eyes when she finished with Dan's wound about fifteen minutes later.

Never before had she witnessed a human soul in such torment. So violently did Dan bite down on the leather that in less than a minute, his teeth had ground clean through it. Frantically, she had torn off another piece of her slip for him to use in place of the leather, and then she had continued to dig at the festering hole in his thigh with her steaming swabs of cloth.

When at last she had begun to see pink, living flesh, she had quit. That was when Dan beckoned her close and with streaming eyes asked if she still had Coleman's gun.

Startled, she admitted she did. He then gave her directions on how to empty the black powder from the caps into his wound. Utterly amazed at what she was doing, a moment later she held a faggot close to the open wound and with trembling hands lit the gunpowder.

It flared brilliantly, and the scream that came from Dan's throat seemed to issue straight from the bowels of hell. A moment later, he lost consciousness, and she set about cleaning the wound once again, then packing it solid with freshly boiled pieces of her dress.

It was much later. Looking back at what she had done, Sharon felt only dim satisfaction that she had managed to clean out that terrible, festering wound. She had no great confidence that the action she had taken would make any difference. After all, she was not a physician. On the other hand, back in Maine she had attended many childbirths alongside competent midwives, and today she had simply followed their teaching on the proper care for unclean wounds. Dan's own drastic remedy with the gunpowder had horrified her, but it did make a certain amount of sense.

After inspecting Dan's bandages one more time, she sat down in a chair, slumped forward onto the table, and closed her eyes. She was slipping over the edge into sleep when the agonizing realization of Tim's death caught her—this time with all her defenses down.

A desolate sense of loss and defeat welled up again from deep within her. She choked back her sobs as best she could, then gave up and let go. She was still crying softly, so as not to disturb Dan, when she fell at last into her own deep, healing sleep.

Chapter 10

S tratemeyer entered the Gold Nugget, spied the sheriff slumped over a bottle, and walked to his table. Without waiting for an invitation, the Pinkerton detective sat down and nodded pleasantly to the groggy lawman. Emory brightened considerably. It was early, and he had cadged his limit of drinks already. Stratemeyer was a good ol' boy who knew how to take care of a buddy.

"How you holdin' up, Strat?" the sheriff inquired, shaking off the effects of booze like a spaniel drying off after a swim.

"Fine, Sheriff. Just fine."

Emory grinned and threw the last of his whiskey down his gullet. "You still ain't had no luck, have you?"

Stratemeyer shrugged his big shoulders easily. "I've had some luck, Emory. The Kid didn't get to keep much of that last gold shipment, did he?"

"You think the Sonora Kid is dead, don't you?"

Stratemeyer nodded. It was true, and he had been acting on that principle. Bill Finney had been hoping the same. The way both of them saw it, who else but the Kid could that have been in O'Hare's office?

Suddenly leaning forward, Emory winked broadly.

"Well, let me tell you something," he said in a hoarse whisper. "Maybe you ain't seen the last of that sonofabitch."

"The last of whom? The Sonora Kid?"

Slowly, portentously, the sheriff nodded, then pushed his empty whiskey glass slyly toward Stratemeyer.

Sitting back in his chair, Stratemeyer studied Emory. What the sheriff had just intimated set Stratemeyer's mind to racing, but he concluded that Emory was too full of booze to make sense. There was no doubt Brett O'Hare and Rafe Barnett—aware that Stratemeyer was onto them— had spirited the dying Kid away and, more than likely, upon his demise had buried him. While Stratemeyer had no easy way to prove Barnett and O'Hare's involvement at this point, that nasty crack on his skull gave him a fine motive for gaining whatever proof he needed. And he did not intend to leave Sonora until he had done just that.

Nevertheless, Stratemeyer couldn't ignore a nagging suspicion that perhaps he was congratulating himself too soon on the demise of the Sonora Kid. If there was one thing the detective knew from long and painful experience, it was that nothing was ever as simple as it appeared on the surface.

"Let me see if I heard you right, Sheriff," Stratemeyer said, sitting up straight. "You say I haven't seen the last of the Sonora Kid. Maybe you better spell that out for me."

"Sure," Emory said, pushing his empty shot glass an inch or so closer to Stratemeyer.

Stratemeyer gave in and called to the barkeep for a bottle. When it came, he filled Emory's glass. The sheriff gulped down the whiskey and slapped the empty glass onto the table, waiting for a refill. When he got it, he downed it just as swiftly, then wiped his bulbous nose and leaned forward, a conspiratorial gleam in his eyes.

"The Sonora Kid is not dead. He will never die!"

Stratemeyer frowned. Was this lush having a fit . . . or delusions perhaps? "You want to repeat that for me?"

The sheriff took a deep breath. "He ain't one man, see?"

"No, I don't see."

"Well, listen then, dammit, while I tell you. The Sonora Kid is not just one outlaw. He is every damn Californio we done wrong to when we crowded in here after this gold! The Sonora Kid will live forever! And the damn Mexes will keep him hid—they'll keep them *all* hid! You're chasin' a ghost, Strat! An' you ain't never goin' to catch him!" He laughed. "You might as well try to capture smoke!"

Stratemeyer sighed. That fresh bottle of whiskey was feeding hot air. So much for what the sheriff knew.

A shadow fell over their table. Stratemeyer glanced up to see Brett O'Hare pausing beside them. His silver hair gleamed and his black mustache was freshly greased.

"Mornin', O'Hare!" boomed the sheriff. "Just been tellin' my buddy here about the Sonora Kid."

"That so?"

"He told me," Stratemeyer said, "that the Kid is not dead."

"An' he ain't never goin' to be," insisted the sheriff, reaching for Stratemeyer's bottle. "It's like tryin' to catch hold of smoke. That's what I told him."

Stratemeyer caught a sudden glint of concern in O'Hare's eyes. Wait. It was more than concern. It was closer to panic. O'Hare looked down with unconcealed irritation at Emory.

"It's pretty early for you to get stinking, ain't it, Sheriff?"

"I am not drunk, sir."

"You're damn close to it as far as I can see." O'Hare turned to Stratemeyer then. "You sure as hell ain't helping matters."

Stratemeyer leaned back in his seat and looked coolly up at O'Hare. "You sure as hell didn't help me much when you lowered that boom on me in Wraither's office, O'Hare."

"I don't know what in blazes you're talking about." A ghost of a smile flickered for just a moment on O'Hare's gaunt face. "Besides, it wasn't me did that."

"Then it was your friend, Barnett."

O'Hare decided to ignore that, and turned his attention back to the sheriff. "Take a walk, Sheriff," he said, his voice laced with contempt. "You're stinking up the place."

With a creaky grin, Emory grabbed Stratemeyer's whiskey bottle and lurched to his feet. "I'll go someplace private," he told O'Hare, "and finish this here nectar of the gods. See you around, O'Hare. Don't call me if you need me."

It is impossible to insult a lush, Stratemeyer thought as he watched Emory stumble out through the batwings, clutching the bottle to his breast the way a mother would her suckling babe. Stratemeyer looked up at O'Hare then.

"You had no cause to light into Emory like that, O'Hare. Something eatin' at you, is it? Something the sheriff just told me, maybe?"

"You come here to drink or gab, Stratemeyer?" O'Hare's voice carried a hint of a threat.

"Hell, you know why I came in here."

Without a word, O'Hare turned and left Stratemeyer's table, heading for his office. Before he reached it, he leaned over the bar and said something to the barkeep, who then glanced over at Stratemeyer and nodded. O'Hare stalked into his office.

Stratemeyer knew without asking that O'Hare had just told the bartender to shut him off. *Interesting*.

With no further reason to stay, he got to his feet and strolled from the saloon. Pausing on the porch, he took a deep breath. He had a lot to mull over. Somehow, what that poor lush of a sheriff had just said struck an exposed nerve in Brett O'Hare. But Stratemeyer just couldn't believe that Emory's words held any truth. Having read the testimony of all the Kid's victims, a Pinkerton-trained detective like himself could come to only one conclusion: The Sonora Kid was one man.

Then what, exactly, was it that had so upset O'Hare?

Stratemeyer breathed deeply again, then walked down the steps to the bustle of Sonora. The banging of hammers filled the bright morning. In addition to the usual construction, a speaker's stand was going up in front of the hotel. Tomorrow was the Fourth of July, and already the air resounded with the snap and bang of the firecrackers the Chinese were selling.

It was difficult at night lately to distinguish the sound of the firecrackers from that of a gun going off. No matter. It added mightily to the air of excitement. Indeed, this Fourth of July promised to be a noisy and spectacular one for Sonora. Already a banner proclaiming the Independence Day festivities had been hung across the main street, and the word passing around was that Colonel Hiram B. Polk would be in attendance and would give an address upon the occasion.

Colonel Polk, Stratemeyer had learned, had gained his fame dispensing justice in the mining camps hereabouts during the early days of the gold strike. At the moment he was a member of the California legislature, and some very powerful and influential voices were already talking him up for governor.

Big doings, then, for Sonora. But as Stratemeyer pushed off the saloon's porch and headed for Bill Finney's express office, he was not thinking so much of the celebration as he was about what had just happened in the Gold Nugget.

Had that inebriate of a lawman stumbled on the truth? *Was the Sonora Kid still alive?*

The makeshift crutch Sharon had fashioned for Dan worked perfectly. He was able to hobble about with some alacrity, and as she watched him now returning from the stream with a full bucket of water, she felt a glow of pride. The morning after the wound had been cauterized, he had awakened without a fever, and from then on his recovery had been gratifyingly rapid.

She attributed this to his hearty constitution and to

her own ability as a cook. She had been filling them both up with the hot soup she concocted from the few cans of beans she found on the shelves and the wild onions and other plants she dug from the stream's marshy banks.

They were both getting sick of this meager fare and had decided it was time to leave. So Sharon had ridden off that morning and found the saddle horse Dan had left in the timber that night when he was following Coleman and Sharon. The poor animal—still encumbered with a saddle—had not strayed far. The moment they had pulled the saddle off its sweating back, the gelding had bucked happily, snorting and wheeling with delight. Now it was grazing in the pasture on the other side of the stream, contentedly cropping the grass alongside Sharon's mount.

They were planning to ride out that afternoon, since Dan insisted he was now fit to ride.

Dan set the bucket down before her. "I could have made it without these crutches," he bragged. "I just didn't want to push it."

For a moment they stood smiling at each other.

"Here. Let me," she said, taking the bucket of water and preceding him into the cabin. As she poured it into the pan on the stove, Dan slumped down on the cot and watched her, his crutch resting on his shoulder.

"I been doing some thinking," he said.

"That's fine," Sharon responded lightly. "Don't get dizzy now."

He smiled. Then he cleared his voice carefully. "It's about that mine you mentioned your brother and his friend were looking for. But if you don't want to talk about it, we won't."

She turned to face him, wiping her hands on the makeshift apron she had fashioned from her chemise. Dan realized the death of her brother was a difficult topic for her to handle; she knew that for this reason he had waited until now to bring it up.

"Go on," she said. "I'm all right."

He took a deep breath. "I think I know where that mine is."

"You do? Where?"

"It's behind that boulder sitting up there on that slope. I'm sure of it. I remember seeing an opening to a mine shaft just before I pulled myself out from behind the boulder. But at the time I had other things on my mind. And besides, I couldn't trust my eyes."

Sharon did not know what to say. If this were true, they might be rich beyond their wildest dreams.

"I seem to remember someone dumping me behind that boulder and telling me that if I recovered, I was never to return to Sonora. If I did, I would be killed."

"It was Rafe Barnett!" Sharon said quickly. "Or that other man with him, O'Hare. One of them must have threatened you. It's their mine." She paused, her expression suddenly bleak. "I told you I was pretty sure one of them murdered Tim. That's why I came here. I was afraid they would kill you, as well."

Dan nodded grimly. "It's obvious they didn't expect me to recover. So I was just left to die. If you hadn't come along, I would have."

"Dan, I think we better get out of here now."

"Not before we explore that mine!"

Sharon considered a moment. Dare they take that chance? But it was a *gold* mine. They would be rich!

"I'll get the candles," she replied with sudden eagerness.

Sharon shuddered unhappily as she pushed through the heavy cobwebs. The candles gave off very fitful light. So far, the steep shaft had shown them nothing of value. Dan seemed impressed, however, with the solid beams used for shoring up the shaft's ceiling and sides.

They turned a corner.

"There!" Dan cried, hobbling swiftly forward on his crutch.

A crude table was sitting along one wall. Under it lay a pick, a sledgehammer, drills, and a shovel—and what appeared to be a barrel of gunpowder. It was the deerskin pouches on top of the table, however, that drew their sustained attention.

Reaching the table first, Dan picked up one of the pouches and hefted it. "It's gold!" he cried. "I can feel it!"

As Sharon bent close, he emptied the pouch carefully out onto the table. Tiny gold flakes gleamed in the candlelight.

Sharon gasped. "I can hardly believe it. How much do you think is here?"

"Enough to make us wealthy," Dan responded quickly. "More than enough."

"Dan, I've been thinking. . . ." She looked up at him. "Won't this be stealing? It will make us no better than they are."

"Maybe so, Sharon. But we'll be taking this gold from two men who were perfectly willing to let me die and one of whom more than likely killed your brother."

"But Tim and his friend were trying to extort them and—"

"That's no excuse for murder."

She argued no further. Secretly pleased that Dan was making it this easy for her, she began counting the pouches. An even dozen in all. She turned away from the table, moving the candle to give her a better view of the shaft. Something on the floor caught her eye.

"What's that?" She started for it.

A depression had been hollowed out of the floor, then lined with boulders. Beside the depression lay three or four long beams with smooth rounded stones attached to each end. In the depression and on the ground around it were scattered pieces of broken and pulverized rock.

"Over here," Dan called. "Look at this."

Dan was standing in front of a wall of stone, from which great chunks had been clawed with picks and in some cases blown out with gunpowder.

"I know what this is," Dan said excitedly, moving his

candle close along the wall. "I read everything about gold mining I could get my hands on before I came out here. This is a quartz vein. That depression in the floor is a Mexican arrastra. Those beams are crude stamping mills used to crush this quartz, freeing the gold embedded in it."

Sharon ran her hand along the rock wall. "This is quartz?"

"Yes. And there's no telling how many ounces of gold it contains. But from the look of those sacks on the table, it is a very rich vein."

In some awe, Sharon stood back and gazed at it.

"I see now why men would kill to keep such a discovery a secret. Can you imagine what that beautiful valley outside would look like once the news of this strike spread?"

"It wasn't concern for the valley that made Rafe Barnett keep this mine of his a secret. It was greed."

"Yes," Sharon said. She looked at Dan then. "And shall we be greedy, too?"

Dan moistened his lips as he considered that question. "No," he said, at length. "We will take just two pouches each and leave the rest. After all, Rafe killed your brother more than likely, and left me to die. It will never be payment enough for what he did, but I think we can take this much with a clear conscience."

Sharon nodded quickly. She felt better at once. "Yes," she said, "we will take that much—and then let us leave this valley quickly, before Rafe Barnett returns."

Belle answered the knock at once. Entering her room swiftly, Manders removed his hat and stepped nervously to one side as Belle closed the door.

"Thank you for seeing me in your room, Belle," Manders said. "This is really very kind of you."

"Nonsense. We're old friends by now, Ted," she said, taking his arm and leading him over to the small table by the window.

He nodded and stuck a finger between his stiff collar

and his neck. His face was red, and perspiration was forming in tiny beads all along his hairline. She did her best not to notice.

As they sat down at the table, she smiled across at him and said, "If I had had a little more warning, I would have had tea sent up."

"No need," Manders said quickly. "No need at all. This is fine."

Belle was trying to be as cool as possible. It was not easy. From the moment the bellhop brought up Manders's note, she realized something was wrong. A gnawing hole seemed to open up in the pit of her stomach while she waited for him to arrive. The note had said simply that he had to see her alone in her room. One glance at the sick, despairing look on his face and she knew at once what he had to see her about.

Just as Belle had suspected—but had tried not to let herself believe—Ted Manders had a wife somewhere. Like a bad penny, she was about to show up.

Manders cleared his throat. He looked like a beached fish gasping for air. She could have helped him begin the discussion, she realized, but she preferred to remain silent.

"Belle," he began, "I have something to tell you."

"Yes, Ted," she said sweetly. "What is it?"

"It's about . . . my wife!"

He blurted the word out so violently that even though she had been prepared for it, Belle was startled enough to draw back.

"I didn't mean to shout," Manders told her, shaking his head in dismay. "It is just that I . . ."

Belle smiled, with just a touch of malice in it. "It's just that you were having such a hard time telling me you were a married man. Isn't that it, Ted?"

He nodded miserably. "I've been meaning to tell you. You don't know how often I have started to tell you . . ."

"I think I knew all along."

"You must hate me."

"Ted Manders, you know better than that!"

"Believe me, Belle, I almost told you after we left the mine the other day, before the picnic. I wanted to tell you then, but . . ."

"I am glad you had the good sense not to," Belle said. "It would have put a damper on a very nice occasion." She smiled then, and this time without any venom. "I had a lovely time."

Manders grabbed both her hands in his. "Belle, so did I! Tell me you forgive me for not mentioning Maud sooner."

"Is that her name? Maud?"

"Yes."

"I forgive you."

He looked deeply into her eyes, searching for some clue that might indicate hidden anger. Then, convinced she was sincere, he smiled slowly and leaned back—a much relieved man. "I do believe you mean that, Belle."

"Of course I do. Now . . . tell me about your wife. Is she on her way here?"

"On her way? She's here now!"

"Already?"

"She arrived this morning. I had no idea she had even left New York. You can imagine what a shock it was for me to answer my door this morning and see Maud standing there!"

"I can imagine," Belle said, unable to keep a smile from her face. "It's a wonder you did not have a stroke."

"I came close to it, I can tell you that." He looked at her then with a sudden, fierce devotion. "You have no idea what your . . . your understanding in this matter means to me, Belle."

She took a deep breath. "Of course I understand. I'm only sorry that things could not have turned out differently." She smiled sadly. "But no matter. We've had fun, Ted. You are a big, gentle man, a pleasure to be with. And I shall always look back at you with love and affection."

"Look back at me! Why, I thought you understood. I

am going to divorce Maud. I have no intention of going back east with her, and besides, Maud is not interested in me. The only reason she has come out here is to check on her share of my wealth. Then she is returning to where—as she puts it—decent people are safe."

Belle could hardly believe her ears. This was not bad news at all, certainly not for her! Ted Manders was married, yes. But soon he would be free.

She leaned back in her chair and looked with deep affection at the big bear of a man sitting across from her. He had thought she would be furious with him for making love to her while still married. And of course, if she had any sense, she would have put on a fine show just now to give that impression. But where Ted Manders was concerned, she could only respond honestly. He had that effect on her.

"Belle? . . ." Manders began uncertainly. "Is there anything wrong?"

"Just let me catch my breath, will you?" she asked. Then she smiled. "Have you any more announcements to make while you're at it?"

He looked mournfully at her and nodded.

"Out with it," she said gently.

"Maud wants me to take her to the mines and then spend the Fourth with her. But afterward, as soon as I can arrange it, I want you to join us for dinner."

"*Dinner?* With you and Maud?"

"Yes! I want her to meet you, and I want you to welcome her to Sonora with me." He hesitated, then plunged on. "Don't you see? It will give her grounds for divorce."

"Ahhhh . . ." Belle understood. "I will be delighted to welcome Maud to Sonora. I shall wear my finest!"

She stood up then. Manders got up also and grasped her arms to draw her near.

"Belle," he said, smiling warmly for the first time since he had entered her room. "Remind me to tell you this more often. But you are some woman. I am a proud and lucky man to have found you."

"Will you please kiss me, and stop all that blather?"

He laughed heartily and opened his arms to her. She stepped closer and felt his arms, strong and warm, folding around her. The moment his lips closed on hers, Belle decided she didn't really want Manders to leave her room—at least not for a while yet.

Chapter 11

Stratemeyer knocked once, then pushed the door open and walked in. Bill Finney was waiting for him behind his desk.

"Got your note," Stratemeyer said. "You have something for me?"

"Sit down," Finney said, indicating with a nod the chair by his desk.

Stratemeyer took off his hat and put it down carefully on the corner of Finney's desk. As he sat down, Finney took his pipe from his mouth and began to clean its bowl with a small jackknife. "You were right," he said, glancing up. "I checked it out. O'Hare doesn't own the Gold Nugget. That Mex who was on the stage with you owns it. Rafe Barnett. O'Hare's his front man."

"How'd Barnett pay for it?"

"Gold dust."

"And now just where do you think he might have got that gold?"

Finney spoke grimly, his eyes blazing with anger. "I been thinking about that, Strat. From robbing my stages!"

Stratemeyer nodded thoughtfully. "Maybe Emory was too drunk to know it, but he was right, after all. The

133

Sonora Kid is not dead. That wounded young Mex Doc Wraither tended in the Gold Nugget might be dead, sure enough. And maybe I killed him. But like O'Hare, he was just a front for the man behind everything."

"Rafe Barnett," Finney said, frowning. "I've heard about him. He's one of those California-born Mexicans, I understand. Californios, they're called. I never laid eyes on him, though. He lives in the Mexican quarter, I'm told, and stays pretty close to the Nugget when he's not there. It all makes sense, Strat, him being behind the Sonora Kid, I mean. That saloon's a perfect place for him to put the gold he takes from my stages into circulation."

Stratemeyer nodded grimly. "When the pieces fit that snug, you might as well put them together."

"Okay, so we put them together. What's next? If Rafe Barnett is the one behind all these holdups—if he's been using the Sonora Kid for his front—shouldn't you arrest him?"

"I have no proof. Nothing I could use in a court of law, that is. Sure, I could haul Doc Wraither in and have him testify about the wounded Mexican Barnett called him in to fix up—and a white jury would waste no time convicting Rafe—if we could keep the Doc sober long enough to testify."

"Then I say do it."

Stratemeyer held up his hand in caution. "On the other hand, Doc Wraither's testimony might not be enough. I've seen juries do some crazy things in my time. And the Gold Nugget has a lot of friends in this town, like the sheriff." Stratemeyer shook his head. "No. That doesn't look like the way to go. Not right now, anyway."

"Then how are you going to stop him?"

"I've already put a crimp in his operation, I figure, by stopping that kid who robbed the stage. Now I'll just have to keep an eye on the Gold Nugget and see if I can't cut them off before their next move."

"Dammit, Strat! That's taking a hell of a chance, ain't it?"

"I'm sorry, Bill. There's nothing else I can do until

they make a move. Since they got back from wherever they buried that Mexican, they've been lying low. But that won't last. Hell, O'Hare already made one mistake when he had the barkeep cut me off. He let me know I was on to something. It was enough for me to ask you to make that check on the Gold Nugget's ownership. Hang in there, Bill," Stratemeyer said gently. "I'll nail this Barnett. That's a promise."

"I hope so," Finney said wearily. "I sure as hell hope so. I still got troubles everywhere I look. A couple days ago, four of my best horses were poisoned. Keep the Kid away from my stages, Strat. I can't take much more."

"I'll do what I can. More I cannot do."

"Aw, hell, I realize that, Strat. I'm just letting you know, is all. I'm about at the end of my rope."

Stratemeyer got up and reached for his hat. "It's getting late. Tomorrow's a big day for Sonora," he said, hoping to lighten the conversation somewhat. "I suppose you'll be up on that reviewing stand listening to all that hot air."

Finney brightened somewhat. "As a matter of fact, I got to give a speech myself. I'll be the one introduces Colonel Hiram B. Polk. That is, I will if that stagecoach of mine arrives on time."

"Maybe I'll see you out there then."

Stratemeyer put his hat on and with a short wave walked out.

Outside the express office building, Stratemeyer paused. The sultry night was filled with the pop and bang of firecrackers, which had increased noticeably with darkness. Children who should have been in bed were tearing along the sidewalks. An electric tension filled the air, as palpable as that preceding a thunderstorm. For these new Californians, the upcoming holiday promised to be a great and momentous occasion. Despite his other preoccupations, Stratemeyer found himself caught up in the excitement along with everyone else.

Still, he would feel a whole hell of a lot better if he

had Rafe Barnett safely put away somewhere. He had talked bravely enough to poor Bill Finney, but Stratemeyer was in a bind. So far, Rafe had been able to keep one giant step ahead of him, and as far as he knew, Rafe was still way out there in front of him.

But perhaps this night he could change all that.

Pulling his hat down so it was a bit more snug, Stratemeyer set off down the street toward the Gold Nugget.

As the last of the young Mexicans filed from his office, O'Hare sat up on the couch and looked across the room at Rafe.

"Did you really have to give them all that gold just to set a few fires?"

"I gave them what I wanted to give them, O'Hare. These past weeks, they've done more for me than set fires."

O'Hare stood up and stretched his long frame. "Ain't no skin off my nose. It's your gold. And I suppose there's plenty more where that came from."

"You can suppose all you want," Rafe told him shortly.

O'Hare nodded, as if he had expected just that response. "Anyway, we are sure as hell going to have an explosive Fourth of July in these parts." He grinned wolfishly at Rafe.

"Independence Day, they call it?" Rafe snapped bitterly. "It is their independence they celebrate—but for me and my people, it means only that the noose grows tighter around our necks. For a century this was the land of our ancestors. We kept it the way we keep a woman we love—with devotion and great care. Our life in this land was a constant, joyous celebration. An Eden we found here, and we kept it so. But now the gringos have it. They rip from its bowels the gold it has and leave in its place nothing but their gringo stench."

O'Hare looked at Rafe. His partner had gone on like this before, and O'Hare should have been used to it. But he could never really get used to such consuming hatred.

"I know it's a foolish question," O'Hare drawled,

more to change the subject than anything else, "but do you still want to move on Stratemeyer tonight?"

"Yes."

"You don't want to hold off a bit?"

"I have held off long enough already! He killed José. Besides, we cannot wait. The man is unpredictable. He prowls about like a big, hungry animal. Already he knows too much, I think. You heard what he told you today. He could ruin what I have planned for tomorrow."

O'Hare shrugged. "Just wanted to make sure, is all."

Rafe looked at O'Hare closely. "You want to pull out, maybe? I will understand. This is not your fight. It was not your wife they hung. And it is not your land they rape."

"No need to get touchy. I was just asking, is all. Count me in."

"All right. I'll count you in. But sometimes, I think maybe you feel too much. You consider too much. For playing poker this is fine, but life is not a game of cards."

O'Hare grinned at Rafe. "You mad at me or something? You sound like my Pa—or maybe my teacher."

Rafe hesitated a moment, then smiled suddenly at his partner. "Enough then. Let us tend to Stratemeyer."

A moment later they left the office. Acknowledging the nods and voiced greetings that came at them from all sides, they disappeared through the batwings into the night.

Watching from a back alley, Stratemeyer saw the four young Mexicans slip out the rear door of the Gold Nugget. He waited until they had disappeared down the alley before slipping through the darkness to the window that looked in on the saloon's office. He was just in time to see O'Hare and Barnett leaving it. Pulling back into the darkness, he waited a while longer, then slowly, carefully lifted the window sash.

He noticed his heartbeat pounding in his ears as he squeezed through the window and stepped into the office. He always felt silly prowling about in another man's home or place of business. A person was really so vulnerable at such times.

Going first to the safe, he did his best to break the combination. The damn thing was too old! The tumblers rattled enough to wake the dead, but told him absolutely nothing. He gave up on the safe and began—very carefully— to go through the big desk.

Only when he found it would he know what he was looking for. He had not lied when he told Finney there was not much hope of making a case before a jury. But if he could find something especially incriminating in this office—an item that just might tip the scales in a court of law—the threat of it could be enough to push Rafe and his partner into a corner.

Cornered rats were dangerous, but they were also vulnerable.

He found just what he needed when he pulled open the bottom drawer of the file cabinet behind the desk: a bloody, silken hood—two holes for the eyes, one for the mouth—and three pieces of jewelry, Sharon Cortland's brooch and Belle Harper's earrings.

Barely able to contain his elation, Stratemeyer wrapped the jewelry in the Sonora Kid's blood-encrusted hood and stuffed it into the side pocket of his frock coat. He straightened slowly, looking around the room to be sure he had left no signs of his entry. Satisfied, he closed the file cabinet drawer and let himself out through the window. Pulling it down all the way behind him, Stratemeyer disappeared into the shadows.

A moment later, the big man emerged from the alley a few buildings down. After dodging aside as two laughing children ran past, he set off briskly along the sidewalk toward his hotel.

As a precaution, Stratemeyer always left a toothpick propped against the door to his room whenever he closed it upon leaving. He approached his door now and out of habit checked for the toothpick. It was not in its place.

Glancing around, he saw it lying flat on the hall carpet almost a foot away. Someone was in his room, waiting.

Without changing his stride, Stratemeyer passed his room and proceeded to the end of the corridor, where he turned the corner. He kept going until he reached a window. After opening it, he stepped out onto the porch roof, then moved cautiously back toward his room. When he had taken the room, he had made sure that at least one window opened onto this roof. He never liked to sleep in a room that had only one exit.

Approaching the corner of the building, he removed his Navy Colt from his cross-draw holster. Then, making sure the moon was not at his back after turning the corner, he dropped to a prone position and inched toward the window. Reaching it, he lifted his head just enough to peer into his room through the narrow opening where his drawn curtains did not quite meet.

The darkness in the room defeated him at first, but he was patient until his eyes adjusted. At last he glimpsed something in the shadows beside his door. The longer he looked, the clearer the form became. Though he could not make out the face, he knew from the figure's slight frame and posture that it was Rafe Barnett. In Rafe's right hand a revolver now caught the moonlight and gleamed dully.

Recalling that he had seen Rafe leaving his office with Brett O'Hare not long before, Stratemeyer's next concern was O'Hare's present whereabouts. The big detective considered a moment. It would not be wise for both of them to wait inside Stratemeyer's room—too crowded. In such close quarters there could be an accident. The best course would be for O'Hare to sit downstairs in the lobby waiting for Stratemeyer to arrive, then follow him up the stairs.

Stratemeyer felt the hair rise on the back of his head. Not once had he looked behind him, and he had left the hallway window open!

Ducking his head down, he turned and was just in time to see O'Hare's lean figure come to a halt on the roof behind him. O'Hare's gun was raised, the long barrel aimed at Stratemeyer's head. Unaccountably, O'Hare held his fire. But Stratemeyer did not hesitate. Rolling swiftly away from the window, he managed to get off a single shot. O'Hare returned his fire, and a searing hot poker slammed into Stratemeyer's head.

Stratemeyer kept rolling and dropped off the roof, coming down awkwardly on the neck of a horse. The collision broke the heavy man's fall and sent the horse rearing. Stratemeyer's head was a bloody mess. Holding it with both hands, he staggered out of the alley and collapsed onto the hotel porch.

The last thing he remembered was a woman's scream and the voice of her companion calling for someone to get Doc Wraither.

Barnett and O'Hare arrived back at the Gold Nugget before word of the shooting reached it. They entered the saloon casually enough and caught sight of Doc Wraither in his customary position: slumped forward onto a table in the far corner.

Rafe paused before the office door and turned to O'Hare. "Stick close to Wraither. Someone will be coming for him soon enough. Find out how bad Stratemeyer was hurt."

Nodding, O'Hare turned and started for the doctor's table. Rafe pushed into the privacy of his own office. Once inside, he swore. Softly. Bitterly. Slumping into his chair, he shook his head. *Mother of God, that was close! What the hell was that big sonofabitch doing on the roof?* Another minute and Stratemeyer would have had the drop on him. O'Hare was a good man to come up on him like that, only it was bad luck he did not kill Stratemeyer for sure. Still, the meddlesome detective was out of action for now—and tomorrow Stratemeyer could do nothing to stop him.

The detonation from O'Hare's gun had sounded like a cannon from where Rafe had waited in Stratemeyer's room. But the firecrackers being constantly set off outside must have lulled everybody else. Bursting from the room, he had met O'Hare coming down the hall. Nobody else was in sight. A moment later the two of them had blended easily into the crowd milling about on the porch.

Now in his office, Barnett looked blankly at the ledger on his desk. After a moment he shoved it away. Now was not the time.

O'Hare returned. Wordlessly, he closed the door, then folded his lean frame down onto the couch. The white-haired man had held up nicely; Rafe was proud of him. But now Brett's face was gray. He looked very sick.

"You did well," Rafe told him.

"That was your idea for me to wait downstairs for him." O'Hare leaned his head against the couch and closed his eyes.

"Yes. With such a man, one cannot be too careful."

"Amen."

"Did anyone come for the doctor?"

O'Hare nodded.

"How bad was Stratemeyer hurt?"

"Looks like he's hurt pretty bad." O'Hare's eyes opened to focus on Rafe. "I caught him in the head. He's out of our way for now. Maybe for good."

Rafe stood up and took a deep breath.

"I think we should ride out now."

O'Hare got slowly to his feet. "Yeah," he said. "Might as well."

Rafe pulled open the bottom drawer of the file cabinet. For a minute he stared foolishly down at the emptiness that yawned beneath him.

"What's the matter, Rafe?"

Rafe turned to look at O'Hare. "Stratemeyer. He was here. In this room. While I waited for him in his room. José's hood is gone, and so is the jewelry."

Joining him, O'Hare stared down at the empty drawer. "I knew we should have dumped that stuff."

"It must be in his pocket now. The hood. And the earrings and brooch. It will make fine evidence . . . if he lives to use it." Rafe kicked the file drawer shut. "It does not matter. We'll ride out tonight and we do not need to come back. I do not need this place anymore. I have other resources."

"That's great. What about me?"

"I will take care of you. Do not worry. Nothing is changed. I'll still meet that stage tomorrow." Rafe smiled. "I have an appointment to keep with the gringo colonel."

Rafe opened the safe and took out ten sacks of gold. Dividing the gold equally between them, the two men gathered up their gear and left the building by the rear door. They were careful to keep within the shadows as they headed for the livery. Their horses, already saddled, were waiting in the stable. As Barnett and O'Hare rode out of Sonora, they passed the hotel. Four men were carrying the big detective inside.

Chapter 12

Rafe and O'Hare rode through the night until they reached the Poker Flats stage way station. In the hills above it, they dismounted, made camp, and slept.

A little after sunrise, O'Hare rode off leading Rafe's mount, while Rafe picked his way on foot through the timber toward the rear of the station. Donning a silk hood he had taken from his saddlebag, he approached the kitchen window. The stationmaster's wife was preparing breakfast. He could smell bacon frying.

A man's voice spoke up, the woman responding. Good—the two were together in the kitchen. Rafe knew from previous visits that there were no small children to complicate matters.

Drawing his revolver, he moved swiftly around to the front door, kicked it open, and entered. The sight of his weapon was enough to intimidate the stationmaster and his wife. The man was in his fifties; his wife, about ten years younger. Both were fat and gringo white, *like maggots*, Rafe was thinking. He told the woman to get some clothesline and tie her husband's hands behind his back. When she finished doing this, Rafe holstered his revolver, inspected her work, then proceeded to tie her hands as well.

He marched them outside and into the timber above the station. There, with two brutal strokes, he clubbed each of them unconscious. Using bandannas he had brought with him for this purpose, he stuffed their mouths and returned to the way station. Then he released the horses from the barn and the corrals and spooked them into the timber with a blanket. He did a thorough job of it before moving into the rocks beside the way station to wait for the stage.

Pulling out a gold pocket watch, he consulted it. He had less than an hour to wait.

Someone had lifted Stratemeyer's head and was pouring raw whiskey down his throat. He was forced to swallow frantically in order to keep up with the flow. It was Wraither. With a clumsy, angry swipe of his arm, Stratemeyer pushed the doctor back from the bed.

The morning sun was pouring through the window, Stratemeyer now realized. It was the next day then, and he was still alive. The brightness was too much for him, and he turned his face away from the exploding daggers of sunlight.

Bill Finney was leaning close. At least it might be Bill, though Stratemeyer could not be sure. A bandage had been wrapped clumsily around the entire right side of his head, including his eye.

"How you feelin'?" Finney asked.

"Like I drank too much. That damn Wraither," he mumbled. "The last thing I need now is his whiskey."

"You're not drunk," Finney assured him. "But you are damn lucky to be alive. You've got a three-inch crease along the side of your head. It's deep enough to leave a permanent scar—but not deep enough to penetrate that thick skull of yours. You must have a doozy of a headache."

"That's right. So don't rock the bed." Stratemeyer winced as he spoke. That bullet of O'Hare's had really rung his bell. He thought of O'Hare then, standing behind him on the roof, his revolver out and fully extended. But why had the man held off like that? Why hadn't he fired sooner, before Stratemeyer turned?

"What the hell happened, Strat?" Finney asked. "Who shot you?"

"O'Hare."

"My God! Why?"

"I'm onto him and Barnett. I have evidence, Finney. All the evidence I need."

"Tell me."

But talking did his headache no good—no good at all. Stratemeyer closed his eyes and looked away from Finney. He was suddenly very, very tired. Must be that damn whiskey Wraither had poured down his throat. "Later," he said.

"All right, sure," Finney said, straightening up and standing back from the bed. "Just lie still for a while. Don't try to talk."

Stratemeyer heard the floorboards creak. He opened his eyes and saw Wraither moving nearer to the bed, peering closely at him, the damned whiskey bottle in his hand. Stratemeyer tried to swipe at him, to keep him back, but the effort was too much for him, and he felt himself slipping into a blessed, healing sleep.

As the Sonora stage pulled up in front of the Poker Flats way station, Colonel Hiram B. Polk stuck his head out the window.

He was a heavy, florid-faced man in his early fifties with a flowing mane of white hair and a yellowing walrus mustache. Dressed in a white linen suit, a black string tie at his neck, and a spotless white broad-brimmed hat, he was looking forward to his scheduled appearance later that day in Sonora. He was to be chief speaker at the Independence Day festivities and had already decided that this would be an ideal opportunity for him to announce his candidacy for governor.

Looking forward to the excitement that such an announcement would generate and eager for the chance it would afford to greet his old friends, the colonel was anxious not to keep his potential voters waiting. Puffing irritably on his cigar, he looked around the empty yard. Not a soul appeared in the station's doorway. And the fresh horses that should have been harnessed and waiting for the stage were nowhere to be seen. He peered over at the corral. Empty. The stage's horses began stamping and blowing in their traces, as impatient as the colonel, it seemed.

Flipping his cigar away in irritation, Colonel Polk yelled up at the Jehu. "Driver! What's the delay? There should be fresh horses ready! I have a speech to give in Sonora! See to it!"

But it was the Fourth of July. On this day there was no strongbox to protect, so the shotgun messenger had been given the day off. He would have taken it off anyway. Wearily, cursing his luck in drawing this day's trip to Sonora, the Jehu climbed down and hurried into the station.

Colonel Polk pulled his head back into the stage. Two other passengers rode with him. One of them, the colonel's secretary, was sleeping in the corner with his mouth gaping open. His name was Wilfred DuBois. A pale thin lawyer recently arrived from the East, he had excellent table manners, but he drank too much and at the moment was in the process of sleeping off last night's excesses.

Beside Polk sat his current lady companion, Sue Ann. Turning to her, he said irritably, "I should have known. Nothing ever gets done properly on holidays."

Sue Ann laughed softly at the colonel's discomfiture. "This is the Fourth of July, don't forget." Then she touched the end of his round, inflamed nose with the tip of her finger. "But that's not fair. Do you really mean that *nothing* got done properly today? On such short notice, I really think I did quite well. Colonel Polk, you hurt my feelings."

Despite himself, the colonel smiled and reached his arm around Sue Ann's ample shoulders. Squeezing her fondly, he said, "No, my dear. Forgive me. I didn't mean that. A woman devoted to her work, such as yourself, never disappoints a . . . a friend."

He had almost said "customer," and she knew it. "I don't know if I like that either," she said with a pout.

Reaching into his pocket, he withdrew a bill and stuffed it into her swelling bosom. Her pudgy fingers plucked it out, and examining the denomination, she exclaimed, "Oh, my!"

"Does that make it any better?"

"Now, you didn't need to do that, Colonel." She leaned over quickly and planted a wet kiss on his mouth. Drawing back for just a moment, she gazed at him, then closed in for another kiss, this time thrusting the tip of her tongue between his lips. She sat back quickly after that and plunged the bill back down between her heavily powdered breasts.

A woman in her early thirties, Sue Ann had a figure that was rapidly getting out of control. The dress she was wearing was cut as low as decency permitted. It was a mixture of black and red, with a nightmarish pattern of lace and other fripperies, which not only exhausted the eye, but expertly hid the fact that she was so heavy in the hip she was developing a tendency to waddle. Her rouged doll's face was as round as a ball, her small cupid lips forever pouting, but her tiny blue eyes were alert and calculating. She was a woman who took a real, almost clinical interest in the more exotic practices of her profession. Such talent made for variety and a kind of cold excitement. She was, as a result, rapidly becoming the colonel's favorite courtesan. He had no qualms at all at being seen in public with her.

The truth of it was the colonel preferred the company of such women to those referred to as the "decent" variety. He had never been able to get satisfaction from a woman without paying for it, and now found he preferred this method to any other. It made things so much simpler. He bought women as he bought everything else.

Wilfred stirred and opened one eye. "Are we there?" he asked, wincing and holding a hand to his head.

"No, dammit!"

The colonel poked his head out the window a second time. The driver was still inside the station. What the hell was going on? Where was the stationmaster?

"Driver!" Polk cried.

The Jehu appeared in the doorway. "There's no one here," he called to the colonel. "I can't figure it out. Maybe it's Indians."

"Hogwash! Get the fresh horses yourself!"

The driver nodded wearily and started off toward the horse barn.

As the frustrated colonel slumped back against the seat, the door to the other side of the stage opened and the Sonora Kid stepped into the stagecoach, carrying a revolver and a heavy coil of rope. Dropping the rope onto the floor, he thrust his revolver's muzzle to within inches of the colonel's face and pulled the door shut. Polk and the others were dumbstruck.

"Do not cry out, *señores, señorita*," the Sonora Kid told them.

The colonel nodded quickly. Sue Ann seemed paralyzed, while all Wilfred could do was stare fixedly at the revolver in the Kid's hand.

The Sonora Kid seated himself beside Wilfred. Clearing his throat, the secretary started to say something, and with calm, impersonal brutality, the Kid clubbed the young functionary on the side of the face with the barrel of his revolver. The force of the blow slammed Wilfred back into the corner of the coach, senseless.

The Kid's eyes returned to the colonel. "Call the driver back. Tell him to forget fresh horses. You don't need them. You have a speech to give in Sonora. Remember, Colonel?"

Amazed, the colonel nodded.

"*Do it! Call him. Now!*"

Thrusting his head out of the stage, the colonel bleated,

"Driver, get back here! I can wait no longer. Drive on! We'll use these horses."

The harried Jehu appeared in the doorway of the barn. He obviously had not understood what the colonel had yelled to him.

"Dammit, Colonel," he cried, "I can't find no horses anywhere!"

"Then get back here and drive on!"

With a weary nod, the Jehu returned to the stage. Colonel Polk leaned his head back against the seat and stared at the revolver in the Kid's right hand. Its muzzle yawned open before him like the mouth of a cannon.

Watching it, he felt cold sweat trickling down from under his armpits. So this was the infamous Sonora Kid. But there was nothing on this stage worth a holdup. And what did he mean by reminding him of the speech he must give in Sonora? This was not an ordinary stage holdup. No, there was something terribly ominous—and frightening—about this highwayman's sudden, inexplicable appearance.

The stagecoach jounced as the driver climbed into his box. A moment later his whip cracked, and the stage lurched forward. When it did, Sue Ann let out a shrill scream. Moving with the speed of a striking rattler, the Sonora Kid slapped her so forcefully she was flung to the floor of the coach. With wide, terrified eyes she stared for a moment at the Kid, then began to weep uncontrollably.

The Sonora Kid looked at the colonel. "If she screams again," he advised him, "I will throw her out of the coach. You had better make sure she knows this."

Colonel Polk nodded quickly, reached out, and drew the weeping woman up to him. Snuffling like an overgrown infant, she reached out and clung to the colonel with a tenacity that threatened to strangle him.

Thinking of the courage Josita had shown in her final moments, Rafe found himself unable to gaze upon this fat bag of gringo garbage. Perhaps he should have pushed her out of the stagecoach in the first place and been done with it. He put this thought out of his mind. He must now act not in anger, but with cool precision. Too long had he waited for this day to let this pig of a gringo woman spoil it for him.

His revolver trained on both of them, he allowed himself to lean back against the seat as the stage rattled on, climbing ever higher—toward the last pass it would have to negotiate before reaching Sonora.

Bill Finney heard his name called and turned to see Jim Coleman's partner pushing toward him through the crush around the speaker's stand. Pleased to see Alexander, Bill shook the old man's hand warmly as soon as he reached him.

"Where's Jim, Alex?" Bill asked immediately. "He's supposed to be up here right alongside the rest of us to welcome the colonel—and the next governor."

"That's why I been looking for you," Alexander replied grimly. He straightened his bent old shoulders and looked Bill squarely in the eyes. "Jim Coleman ain't gonna be here—not today, not ever. Jim's dead, Bill. His body's in my wagon back at the store."

Finney felt his knees go weak. A sudden premonitory fear swept through him. "My God, Alex. What are you saying? Jim dead? How?"

"Can we go someplace to talk?"

Bill led Alexander through the crowd and up onto the hotel porch to a reasonably quiet spot at the far end.

"Jim got himself into a peck of trouble," Alexander began. "He tried to rape that Cortland girl."

At first Finney felt outrage . . . shock. Then came a weary dismay. He wanted to find it difficult to believe, but he didn't.

"Go on," he said grimly.

"According to her, there was a struggle on the trail in the middle of the night. She shot him, and Jim fled. I was on my way back here with the wagon when some miners working Johnson Creek stopped me. They'd just found Coleman's body floating face down in the shallows."

"You mean this girl killed Coleman?"

"He had a gunshot wound, sure enough. But it wasn't nearly enough to kill him. Coleman drowned, Bill. Another thing, most every bone in his body was broke. I figure he fell an awful long way into that creek. That might've been what killed him, too."

"He was so damn scared when that woman shot him, he plunged off a cliff in the dark. Is that what you're saying?"

"I'm saying that's the kindest way of looking at it. Them miners at Pine Hill already know why that Cortland woman was alone when she delivered their goods and mail to the diggings. They know 'cause I told 'em. But now I figure the best thing is to leave it that he took a long step in the dark and drowned."

Finney considered for a moment, then nodded. "All right. I'll back you on that. Makes sense, I suppose."

Alexander nodded, his old, seamed face suddenly very grim. "Course you understand, Bill, there ain't no one who really knows for *sure* how Jim Coleman died. And that's the way it is going to have to be."

"Yes, Alex. I understand that."

"Good."

With a quick nod, the old man turned and walked off the porch. He was in his late seventies, Finney knew for a fact. But he moved as spryly as a young lad in springtime.

Again Finney heard his name called. The mayor was beckoning to him from the crowd of potentates bunching up behind the speaker's stand. Deciding to say nothing about what he had just learned until after the festivities, Finney waved back to the mayor and hurried off the porch toward him.

But as he plunged back into the festive, back-slapping crowd, he found himself unable to dispel the sense of doom that now seemed to hang over the day's celebration.

Less than three miles from Sonora, Wilfred stirred groggily and then came awake. With the same casual brutality he had shown earlier, Rafe clubbed him again into insensibility and then looked out the window. Yes—

O'Hare was now galloping along behind the stagecoach, keeping about a quarter of a mile back, with Rafe's horse on a lead behind him.

Ducking back inside, Rafe reached over and pulled the whore away from the colonel. She began to whimper. He brought the barrel of his revolver down on her head, but she just blinked and sat back, staring wide-eyed at him, too terrified to scream.

Mother of God, he said to himself, and struck her again, harder. This time she slumped unconscious into the corner of the stage. Rafe took off his hood and flung it to the floor of the stage.

"Look at me, Colonel Polk," he said. "Do you remember me?"

Close to panic, the colonel shook his head quickly. "What do you mean? Why should I know you? Of course I don't!"

"Are you sure, Colonel?"

"Yes! Dammit!"

"Look closer. Two years ago. The American Creek camp. Josita Escobar. She had no honor to protect, remember? To you she was only a Mexican whore!"

Staring incredulously at Rafe, Colonel Polk slumped back against his seat.

"You . . . Escobar!"

"Yes! Rafael Escobar! I have not forgotten, Colonel. All this time I have remembered—even if you have not."

"It was a trial! A fair trial!"

Rafe raked the barrel of his revolver across the colonel's face, leaving a deep, puckering gash from cheekbone to cheekbone. The colonel's red, bulbous nose was reduced to a bloody smear.

He began to whimper.

Ignoring him, Rafe reached down for the rope. He had already fashioned the hangman's noose. Dropping it over the blubbering colonel's head, Rafe tightened it with one quick pull. Thrusting his revolver into his belt, he leaned out through the coach window and looped the rope around the baggage rack. Pushing the coach door open slightly, he snubbed the rope around the door jamb and knotted it. The rope had already been cut to the proper length. It was short enough to do the job without trailing so far behind the coach it would attract the Jehu's attention.

During all this, the colonel offered no resistance or protest. He simply remained crouched in the corner, whimpering, the rope hanging from his neck.

"Colonel Polk," Rafe said, leaning close to the terri-fied man. "Listen to me, Colonel Polk. I want you to tell this Jehu to go faster. Tell him you are late. Tell him if he does not get you to Sonora in time, you will have him fired!"

The colonel stopped whimpering. Hope gleamed in his eyes. But he was still too terrified to move.

"Tell him, dammit!" Rafe snarled. "Tell him or I'll push you out!"

At once this threat aroused the colonel. Panting in terror, he plunged past Rafe and poked his head out the window.

"You must go faster!" he called up to the Jehu. "Faster! I must be on time!"

Rafe could barely hear the driver responding, but he seemed to be protesting.

"I will have you fired!" the colonel cried. "Faster, I tell you! I must get there in time."

Rafe heard the Jehu cursing, after which came the sharp crack of his whip. He kept it cracking, and the coach's speed increased measurably. The colonel ducked back inside the coach and turned to stare at Rafe. His face was as full of hope as a child's at Christmas.

"There!" he cried. "You see! We won't be late. Soon we will be in Sonora!"

"No . . . you won't," said Rafe, kicking open the door.

The colonel glanced in terror at the flapping door, then back at Rafe. "What are you doing?"

"I am going to do what you did to my Josita."

"But you said—" The colonel's hands flew up to the rope around his neck. For a moment it appeared he was going to cry. "Please! We will soon be in Sonora! You must not do this!"

"Beg all you want, Colonel. I have waited a long time to hear you beg. Now you will die like the gringo coward you are, stinking up the air with your bleating!"

"No, no! Wait! I will give you anything! Soon I will be governor!"

Rafe leaned forward, his eyes suddenly alight, as if this news had great significance.

"Oh? Is that true, Colonel?"

"Yes!"

"Of California?"

"Yes!"

"You are wrong, Colonel Polk! You will be governor only of hell!"

Rafe grabbed the colonel's shoulder and spun him out through the door. The colonel struck the ground just inches from the rear wheels, then vanished from sight. The rope snapped taut.

Rafe waited to see if the Jehu had noticed anything, but the whip was still cracking, urging the team on with undiminished urgency. To save his job, he was determined to get to Sonora in time.

Peering back down the roadway, Rafe caught sight of O'Hare just beyond the rooster tail of dust. The colonel must be suffering greatly, Rafe thought. He smiled, leaned out of the coach, waited for a good spot, then dropped from the stage. As soon as he struck ground he rolled to cushion his fall and came erect unhurt. O'Hare was reining in beside him a moment later.

"You took your time!" O'Hare cried. "We're almost to Sonora!"

Without replying, Rafe swung into his saddle. Then he grinned at O'Hare.

"Come! Now we watch Sonora burn!"

The mayor was rushing down the street, waving his arms at the band. At once it began to play.

"Here she comes!" someone bellowed from the far end of the street. "Here comes the stage!"

Finney glanced at his pocket watch in some irritation, then reached down to help the mayor up onto the speaker's stand. The crowd in front of the stand turned to greet the incoming stage—and its famous native son, Colonel Hiram B. Polk.

"He's probably got one of his floozies with him," the mayor said out of the corner of his mouth.

"Why, that's part of Colonel Polk's charm," responded Finney.

The stage turned onto the main street, the Jehu standing up in the box to rein in his hard-charging team. *He must have been driving them full out,* Finney realized, wincing at the thought. He couldn't afford to lose another team.

The band was blowing furiously by now, and the crowd was cheering. Suddenly from someone in the crowd lining the street came a high, keening scream. As the stage swept on toward the speaker's stand, the spectators on the sidewalks broke ranks and rushed after it, pointing to something dragging in the dust just behind its right wheel.

Only when the stage pulled to a rattling halt in front of the stand did Finney see what had been dragging behind it. It was the body of a man!

"The colonel!" someone in the street cried. "It's the colonel!"

Rushing from the stand, Finney pushed his way through the crowd and knelt beside his old acquaintance. What he saw sickened him. The colonel had been wearing a white linen suit; now what was left of it clung in dark bloody tatters to his torn frame. In places the colonel's skin hung from his carcass in blackened, dirt-encrusted strips. And his face was a raw, pulverized mass—with one long gash across its front.

Incredibly, the old campaigner was still alive, and his hands clutched viselike around the noose strangling him. Opening an eye, he saw Finney.

"Colonel!" Finney cried, leaning close and quickly loosening the noose. "Who did this?"

The colonel's mouth worked convulsively, but nothing came. The colonel's blackened tongue was so swollen it almost filled his mouth.

Leaning still closer, Finney said urgently, "Tell us! You must tell us, colonel! Who did this to you?"

He rested his ear against Polk's mouth. The colonel began to move his lips once again. The crowd hushed. In a whisper so faint it seemed to come from another world, Finney heard a name that froze the blood in his veins.

"Rafael Escobar!"

Chapter 13

Stratemeyer saw the colonel die from his hotel window. The crowd's expectant cheer and the sudden explosion of brass from the band in the street below his room had aroused him, but it was the screaming that caused him to throw aside his bedcovers and rush to the window. Doc Wraither was sleeping it off in a corner and stirred not an inch as Stratemeyer flung up the sash and leaned out.

He was in time to see the stagecoach pull to a halt in the midst of the crowd. As he watched, Bill Finney leaped from the speaker's stand and pushed through the crowd. But what all the commotion was about eluded Stratemeyer until he caught a glimpse of the bloody torso that had just been dragged into Sonora behind the stagecoach.

At almost the same instant that Bill Finney stood up and bowed his head over the dead colonel, Stratemeyer saw something else just as dismaying. Pulling himself back into the room, he hurried over to the other window and shaded his eyes in order to see more clearly. Though as yet undetected by the crowd below him in the street, a roaring tower of flame was building up in the yard behind Bill Finney's express office. Seconds later, with a muffled

roar, the roof of the express office itself dissolved into a
billowing mass of smoke and flames. A shower of glowing
embers shot high into the air.

It was this that alerted the crowd below. For a moment everyone in the crowd turned as one and stood
frozen. Then, as cries of "Fire!" rent the air, the people
began racing in the direction of Finney's office and stables.

Stratemeyer flung himself into his clothes. He had
some difficulty getting his hat on over his bandaged skull,
but he managed somehow and, ignoring the dull, persist-
ent ache, rushed from the room.

It was late that afternoon. Stratemeyer and Bill Finney
were in the hotel dining room, trying to slake their massive thirst and to get something to eat. Like the many
other smoke-begrimed fire fighters who filled the place,
both men were near total exhaustion.

By dint of a truly prodigious effort, they—along with
practically every other able-bodied townsman—had managed to save most of Sonora's business district. From the
beginning, though, there had been no chance at all of
saving the buildings that made up Bill Finney's stagecoach
line and hauling business. Even more tragic was the loss
of so much of his livestock. Finney had been able to save
only five horses.

He was ruined.

Stratemeyer was not exactly surprised, therefore, when
Finney seemed less than elated at Stratemeyer's news
concerning Rafe Barnett. The testimony of the colonel's
two gruesomely battered companions on the stage—together
with the silken hood and the stolen jewelry Stratemeyer
had found earlier in the Gold Nugget office—was all the
evidence he needed to arrest and hang Rafe Barnett.

Finney looked bleakly across the table at Stratemeyer.
"Fine," he said in a flat, emotionless voice. "The Gold
Nugget was burned to the ground. There has been no sign
of Barnett or O'Hare and little likelihood that either one
will turn up soon. Do you know where they are? When do
you think you'll be bringing Rafe in for his trial, Strat?"

"Soon enough."

Finney smiled. It was a terrible, mirthless smile that revealed only a fathomless despair. "No, you won't. But it doesn't make any difference, none at all. What happened today is God's judgment. I saw it coming, but I refused to admit it to myself. I can deny the truth of it no longer."

"What the hell are you talking about, Bill?"

"Do you know who placed that hangman's noose around Colonel Polk's neck and flung him from that stage?"

"I just told you. We've got the testimony of those two who were in the stagecoach with the colonel. It was the Sonora Kid—so that means it was Rafe Barnett."

"No, Strat. It was Rafael Escobar. Before the colonel died, that was the name he gave me. They were his dying words."

"Who the hell is Rafael Escobar?"

"The husband of a woman we lynched two years ago."

Stratemeyer suddenly leaned back in his chair. "Oh my God. . . . Where was this?"

"In a mining town north of here. It has since been abandoned, but that isn't important. What is important is that Escobar swore he would kill those of us he felt were most responsible for his wife's hanging. And with the exception of myself, he has done just that. During this past year, four men, including the hangman, died violent or suspicious deaths."

"You don't suppose that could have been a coincidence."

"I wish I could believe that, Strat. But I don't. Listen. Jim Coleman provided his wagon that night, and he was the one who whipped the horses that left Josita Escobar hanging. A little while ago, Strat, some miners working Johnson Creek found Jim Coleman. He was floating face down in the shallows. He had a bullet wound, but that was not what killed him. He'd been thrown from a great height." Finney smiled then, only it was more like the grin on a death's-head. "Now Polk is dead. He was the sixth to die. I will be the seventh."

"No, you won't, dammit! Stop talking like that."

"Why, Strat? Why not admit the truth? What do I have to live for? And even more important, why should I outlive all those men? I was no less guilty than they were." Finney leaned closer to Stratemeyer, his voice taking on a new urgency. "Do you think I have been able to forget that terrible night—or the sight of that woman calmly taking it upon herself to adjust the hangman's noose around her neck? She haunts my dreams still. And I haven't forgotten Rafael Escobar's anguish. I tied his hands behind him so he would not interfere. My God, Strat! Is it any wonder that he singled me out for this slow death— robbing my stages, poisoning my stock, wrecking my equipment, burning me out—after what I did?"

"Easy now, easy," Stratemeyer said, in an effort to soothe the man. "It wasn't all your fault. You can't take it all on yourself."

"Strat, I knew Rafael and Josita! I was friendly with them! When the trial first began, Escobar looked to me as a friend, someone who might be able to talk some sense into that drunken mob of miners!"

"It's over now."

"Not yet, it isn't. My turn is coming."

"Cut that talk, Bill."

"No, I mean it, Strat. I'll be number seven."

Stratemeyer leaned back in his chair and shrugged, defeated. Finney simply refused to be comforted. When the food they had ordered arrived, they ate a little; but despite their earlier exertions, neither man could muster much of an appetite.

Gently, so as not to open too many old wounds, Stratemeyer asked for more details on Jim Coleman's death. Finney told him what he knew about it.

"So as you can see, it was not the Cortland woman who killed him," Finney said at the last. "It was Rafael Escobar—Rafe Barnett."

"He sure as hell gets around."

"Yes, he does."

And that ended the discussion. After a decent interval, they both quit picking at the food in front of them and finished their coffee. Excusing himself wearily, Finney left money on the table to cover his check and retired to his room. His living quarters had been on the floor above his office. He would stay at the hotel now.

A few moments later, Stratemeyer strode out onto the hotel's wide front porch and found a chair. The porch and street were nearly empty. For a Fourth of July, the afternoon was startlingly quiet, which was understandable. The fire had exhausted the townspeople. They had had enough fireworks for one day. Those who had homes left had fled to them, and those businessmen who, like Finney, had been wiped out were gathering in saloons and offices, planning the rebuilding that would have to start as soon as possible. Meanwhile, the stench of burning things still hung oppressively in the air.

Stratemeyer lit a cigar. He had found Finney's story a remarkable one. It caused him to regard Rafe Barnett— Rafael Escobar—in a new light. Barnett was no longer just another highwayman bent on robbing stagecoaches to line his pockets. He had had other, darker motives. Stratemeyer shook his head. Once again he was forced to admit that nothing was ever as simple as it seemed at first.

He leaned back in his chair, pondering his next move. Finney was right, of course. It was not going to be a simple matter to bring in Rafe Barnett. He and O'Hare had not been in Sonora since the night before. Meanwhile, the Gold Nugget, their base of operations, had been gutted by the very fire they or their accomplices had set. By this time they must know that they were finished in this town—and they were most likely fleeing the area.

Abruptly, the town's oppressive silence was shattered by the heavy crump of a shotgun. The explosion came from a room in the hotel directly above the chair in which Stratemeyer was sitting.

Flinging away his cigar, Stratemeyer bolted into the hotel lobby. The roar of the shotgun's blast had momentarily frozen everyone there. Guests were staring at each other uncertainly. Stratemeyer went straight to the desk clerk.

"I want Bill Finney's room number!" he said.

"Twelve. On the second floor, front."

Stratemeyer took the stairs two at a time. When he came to room number twelve, he didn't stop. With a well-placed kick, he sent the door slamming back against the inside wall. Rushing in, he found Bill Finney—very much dead. Like a Roman falling on his sword, he had tucked the muzzle of a sawed-off shotgun into his stomach, leaned forward to steady it, then reached down with his thumb to the trigger.

Feeling sick at the gruesome finality of the scene, Stratemeyer returned to the hallway, where a crowd was rapidly gathering outside the room. Pulling the door shut behind him, he pushed through the curious onlookers and headed for the lobby.

Halfway down the stairs, he met the distraught hotel manager on his way up. He asked Stratemeyer what had happened.

"Bill Finney just made it seven," Stratemeyer responded to the bewildered man, and kept on going.

Belle was crossing the hotel lobby on her way up to her room when she heard a familiar voice call out her name. Turning, she saw Sharon Cortland and a drawn, weary Dan Prentiss entering the hotel.

Hurrying across the lobby, Belle embraced her friend warmly and then smiled with some concern at Dan.

"You look somewhat peaked, young man," she observed.

"He was hurt fearfully," Sharon said. "But he's going to be all right, and oh, my, do we have a story to tell! But not now . . . later."

Belle smiled. "All right, then. Later. And I'll hold you to that."

"Belle," Sharon went on, "we could hardly recognize Sonora. It must have been a terrible fire! We could smell the smoke miles from town."

"The stage line's gone, too, I see," said Prentiss. "That's too bad. We were planning on taking it back to San Francisco."

Sharon brightened then. "Dan and I are getting married. We're going to stay at a fine hotel in San Francisco and have a real honeymoon!"

"Aha!" said Belle. "So that's the story you have to tell."

"It's more than that," Sharon said, dropping her voice suddenly and leaning close to Belle. "We're rich, Belle!"

"Rich? You mean *gold* rich?"

Sharon nodded quickly, eagerly. "But you mustn't breathe a word. Now, what about you? How have you been doing?"

Belle laughed softly. "I think I've been doing very well. But for the moment I will have to wait before I count my chickens. They have not yet hatched."

"Is it about that fellow who took you to breakfast? Is he the one?"

"Yes."

"Oh, that's wonderful, Belle! He is such a big, handsome man."

Belle smiled wryly. "He is that. And soon, I am to meet his wife."

Sharon's face fell. "Oh, Belle!"

Belle reached out and took Sharon's arm. "We'll talk about it later. Not here. Now check into your rooms and freshen up. I am supposed to keep myself discreetly hidden for now, so why don't you come up to my room after dinner."

"Yes, I will! We have so much to talk about!"

Belle said good-bye and left them. As she mounted the stairs a moment later, she looked back at the two of them and waved, wishing she felt as confident as she tried to appear to them.

Stratemeyer, on his way back from the funeral parlor, was just entering the hotel when he saw Belle leaving Sharon and Dan Prentiss. Remembering that he had in his coat pocket the jewelry that belonged to Sharon and Belle and some money in the hotel safe that belonged to Prentiss, he sat down in a lobby chair and waited for them to check in. Then he got up and walked over to them.

Sharon recognized him at once, as did Prentiss. She looked breathless and excited, Stratemeyer thought, if perhaps a bit weary. Prentiss, on the other hand, did not appear to be well. In fact, he looked just about as bad as Stratemeyer felt. The suicide of Bill Finney following hard on the heels of a fiercely destructive fire had done nothing for Stratemeyer's pounding head.

Suggesting it might be best if they could talk in private, Stratemeyer ushered them over to a quiet corner of the lobby, where they found a sofa and upholstered chairs. Dan seemed particularly grateful for the opportunity to slump down on the sofa and relax. He had evidently been through a lot in the past week.

"Mr. Stratemeyer . . ." Sharon said, sitting down beside Dan as she peered at the detective's smoke-blackened bandage. "You've been hurt! Was it the fire?"

"No, it wasn't," Stratemeyer told her. He sat down in a soft chair near the sofa and smiled. Reluctant to explain his injury further, he said, "Well, I must admit, you seem quite happy and excited."

"Oh, I am! Dan and I are getting married!"

"We're going to San Francisco for our honeymoon," Dan said.

This news did not surprise Stratemeyer. The two were perfectly suited to each other. "Congratulations," Stratemeyer told Sharon. "As it happens, I have something for you. Consider it a wedding present."

Reaching into his side pocket, Stratemeyer drew forth Sharon's emerald brooch. Leaning over, he handed it to her.

"Why, it's my brooch! Oh, thank you!" she cried, astonished.

"I remember you were quite upset when the Sonora Kid took it from you. And your future husband suffered a mean crack trying to get it back for you."

"But however did you get it?"

"From the gentleman who stole it from you, of course."

"You caught him? You caught the Sonora Kid?"

"Not exactly. But that's another story. I really should keep the brooch for evidence. But I couldn't resist giving it to you just now."

"Oh, I'm so glad you did. You have no idea what this means to me."

Stratemeyer again reached into his pocket. "Will you be seeing Belle Harper soon, Miss Cortland? She probably would like to have these. . . ." In his hand were the earrings the Sonora Kid had taken from Belle.

"I'll be glad to give them to her, Mr. Stratemeyer. She'll be most grateful to you, just as I am."

Turning to Prentiss then, Stratemeyer told him that his five hundred dollars was waiting for him in the hotel safe. Prentiss beamed.

Stratemeyer cleared his throat nervously and looked back at Sharon. "There's just one more thing, Miss Cortland. It concerns you. You've got to be told, and I figure now's as good a time as any."

They both caught the deep concern in his voice. "Yes, Mr. Stratemeyer," Sharon said, "what is it?"

"Jim Coleman's dead."

Sharon's hand flew up to her mouth, her eyes widening in horror. Prentiss put both arms around her shoulders to comfort her.

"Good," Prentiss snapped. "Coleman deserved to die!"

"Perhaps," Stratemeyer said wearily. "The thing is, Miss Cortland, you did not kill him."

"But I shot him. . . ."

"We know that. But it was not your bullet that killed him."

"Then who did?"

"Someone a little while ago suggested it might be the man you know as Rafe Barnett."

The two exchanged a sudden, furtive glance. Prentiss hesitated for an instant, then nodded to her. Sharon turned back to Stratemeyer and cleared her throat.

"Mr. Stratemeyer," she said. "I think Rafe Barnett killed my brother, Tim."

Stratemeyer frowned. "I am sorry to hear of your brother's death, Miss Cortland. But why do you believe Barnett is responsible?"

Prentiss spoke up then. "Tim was after Rafe Barnett's mine."

"But we found it," Sharon said, her eyes suddenly gleaming with thinly veiled avarice.

"And we can go there anytime and take what we want," said Prentiss. "It sure don't look like Barnett filed any claim on it."

"You've found Ali Baba's cave, is that it?"

Sharon nodded emphatically. "Yes. And why not? After all, he killed my brother!"

"And he and his partner left me to die," Prentiss said angrily. "It was Sharon here who saved me."

Stratemeyer frowned. "A mine you say?"

"Yes," Prentiss replied. "It is fairly well hidden in a valley north of here. Barnett has a small cabin there."

"I will want directions to that valley. Come up to my room with me now while I get my gear ready."

Sharon frowned in protest. "But . . ."

"No buts," Stratemeyer snapped. "I want Rafe Barnett, and I don't give a damn about any hidden mine you two are so greedy to keep for yourself. Is that clear?"

Chastened, Sharon and Prentiss nodded. Stratemeyer got to his feet, and with no further argument, the silent couple followed him up the stairs to his room.

Rafe knew something was amiss when he saw the hoofprints outside his cabin. Dismounting swiftly, he entered. One glance and he knew he had had visitors—visitors who had stayed awhile. The place was clean enough. Too clean. The cot was made neatly, and the floor was swept. Looking up at the shelves, he saw that the cans of beans he had stored there were missing, and on the stove the pot had been scrubbed to a sheen.

A woman's touch.

Following wearily in behind him, O'Hare came to a halt in the doorway and watched Rafe's swift, agitated inspection of the place. "What's the matter, Rafe?"

"Someone's been here," Rafe snapped. "A woman, more'n likely."

O'Hare shrugged. "Place don't look so bad. Real clean, as a matter of fact. Why complain?"

"I don't like visitors to this valley."

"Yeah, I know. There's José's grave and all. But you don't own this valley, Rafe, and sooner or later you're going to have visitors."

"I would rather it later, not sooner."

O'Hare walked past Rafe and slumped onto the cot. Kicking off his boots, he folded his arms under his head. "That was a long ride. I'm going to get some sleep."

Rafe glanced at him, then nodded. "I am going out," he said.

O'Hare grunted a reply and shut his eyes.

Rafe found the first piece of bloodstained bandage on the trail leading up to the burial site. When he bent closer to the ground, he noticed how the grass was still matted in places, matted with dried blood. Then he saw the gouges in the soft ground. Something sharp had been dragged over it. A stick? Or perhaps the tip of a boot. But whose boot? He realized then that Brett must have dragged the dead Prentiss to his grave. Relieved, he continued along the wavy furrow to the burial site . . . but the trail didn't stop there.

Rafe felt a stab of panic. Things were not right—first the cabin and now this. Climbing slowly along the trail, Rafe found himself getting closer to the boulder that marked his mine.

Reaching it, he saw at once footprints so heavy that they had obliterated some of the grass. Behind the boulder he glimpsed another bloody piece of bandage. He snatched it up. So O'Hare had stashed Prentiss here, Rafe was thinking, *while the fool dug an empty grave*.

But he needed to make sure. Galloping back down the slope, Barnett returned to the cabin, grabbed the

shovel leaning against the outside wall, and hurried back
up the mountainside to the burial site. The ground above
the grave alongside José's was still soft, the fresh, gravelly
dirt forming a slight mound.

Swiftly, Rafe plunged the shovel into the fresh earth.
He dug with cold fury for at least five minutes, not striking
anything but the rocks O'Hare had placed just under the
surface. He flung the shovel down. No longer did he have
any doubt at all: *O'Hare had tricked him.*

A cold, paralyzing thought occurred to him then.

Without glancing back at the grave, he hurried up the
slope to the boulder and ducked in behind it. At the mine
entrance, he reached up for a candle resting on a beam
and lit it with a sulfur match. Striding so quickly down the
sloping shaft that the candle was almost extinguished, he
turned the corner.

The last time he was here, Rafe had left the table
piled high with twelve deerskin pouches containing all he
had been able to mill from the quartz vein. Now the pile
was not so high. That any pouches were left at all astonished him, and he hurried over and counted them—eight.

And then he smiled.

Those who had robbed him would return for the rest
when they could no longer contain their greed. But when
they did, they would find nothing! He would see to that.

Entering the cabin a few minutes later, Rafe closed
the door softly and lifted his revolver from his belt. Cock-
ing it, he approached the cot where O'Hare was sleeping.
The man had turned to the wall. His quiet, steady breathing filled the cabin. Lifting a chair silently, Rafe set it
down beside the cot and straddled it, resting his arms on
the back.

O'Hare had to die for betraying him. The fool had not
killed Dan Prentiss, and it was Prentiss—in league with
that blond woman, Rafe had no doubt—who had stayed
here and looted his mine. By hiding Prentiss behind that
boulder, O'Hare had unwittingly revealed the opening to
his mine.

Rafe aimed the revolver carefully, coolly, letting the

sight center on a spot just below the juncture of the head and spine. At this distance, the round would sever O'Hare's spinal column.

Rafe sighed deeply.

He knew why O'Hare had not killed Prentiss. Just as O'Hare could not kill that miner who challenged him earlier this week, he had found himself unable to pull the trigger on Prentiss. Compassion. Brett O'Hare—this partner of his for so long—had been rendered useless by his compassion for his fellowmen. And now he was lying here helplessly asleep, as if eager for Rafe to kill him.

Slowly, Rafe uncocked his revolver and returned it to his belt. Standing up silently, he replaced the chair alongside the table.

"O'Hare!" he called.

O'Hare stirred. Rafe called his name a second time, louder. Shaking his head, O'Hare turned around and sat up. As he blinked up at Rafe, he managed a grin.

"I'm starved," he said. "Let's get a fire going."

"No, O'Hare. You will ride out. Now. If I ever see you again, I will kill you."

O'Hare had difficulty digesting Rafe's words. "What the hell, Rafe? You gone loco, or something?"

"It is you who are crazy, amigo. You have this fool compassion for others—despite all you know about them. You let Prentiss live. I do not understand. But now I wash my hands of you."

O'Hare's eyes narrowed in sudden comprehension. "You mean the sonofabitch lived? Hell, I'm sorry, Rafe. I just couldn't pull the trigger on him."

"Get your gear and ride out!" Rafe leveled his weapon once again at O'Hare. "Do it now, O'Hare, before I change my mind."

"Go ahead. Change your mind. Shoot me. You'd be doing me a favor, Rafe."

Rafe smiled coldly. "I know that, O'Hare. You are a strange man. You cannot kill those who deserve to die, yet you seek death. It is for that reason I did not shoot you while you slept."

With a weary shrug, O'Hare moved past Rafe and out to his horse. Still covering him, Rafe watched him mount up. Then he pointed to the other end of the valley.

"Go that way—to the northeast. And keep going. I warn you. If I see you again, I will kill you."

O'Hare touched the brim of his hat in salute, then spurred his mount up the valley. Rafe followed after him a ways, watching with some regret as the slim man rode off into the deepening night; then he shoved his revolver back into his belt. He was glad he had not shot the gringo. The man hated the punishment of living. To have killed him would have rewarded him for his weakness—and would have given Rafe no pleasure.

The next morning, Rafe was very busy. Using the long branch he had used to lever the boulder in place before the mine entrance, he sent the boulder crashing at last down the slope. Gaining a fearsome momentum, the boulder bounded over a few ridges, splashed through the creek, and came to rest finally against a knoll on the far side of the valley.

Taking what gold was left from the mine, Rafe stashed it in his saddlebags. The black powder he had used for blasting into the quartz vein he used now to blow up the mine itself. The explosion was a titanic one. From a safe distance away, Rafe watched as the face of the mountain slope directly above the mine appeared to shift massively downward, obliterating the mine entrance entirely.

The area around the mine entrance now wholly unrecognizable, Rafe rode to his cabin and poured coal oil liberally over the floor and walls. Then walking outside, he fashioned a torch from an old shirt and some kindling. Striking a match, he lit the torch and threw it inside. With a shuddering *whump* the cabin's interior became a sheet of flame.

Standing a good distance from the cabin as he watched it burn, Rafe felt a deep satisfaction, as if the fire was burning out of him the last vestiges of the bloodlust that had driven him for so long. In wiping out all trace of the mine and destroying his cabin, he was seeing to it that this valley—unlike so many other equally lovely valleys—would not be despoiled by the heedless, debauching gangs of forty-niners who had already fouled so much of his fair California.

Having ridden through the night, Stratemeyer was just entering the pass when a muffled explosion ahead caused him to pull up. Deciding it would be best not to ride openly into the valley, he started up again, this time following a game trail that took him along the mountain's flank high above the valley floor. At the last, he was guided by a black pillar of smoke climbing almost straight up into the late afternoon sky.

Coming out just above the burning cabin, he saw Rafe Barnett standing some distance from the flames, his back to Stratemeyer, a saddled horse standing beside him. Dismounting, Stratemeyer tied his horse to a sapling and angled down the steep slope toward Rafe.

In the fire's roar, his footfalls were inaudible. And Rafe seemed to be lost in his contemplation of the inferno he had created. Stopping a few feet behind him, Stratemeyer cocked his revolver.

This sound Rafe heard.

Spinning, he saw the detective. For a moment his face showed nothing. Then the man smiled. "You are a big, slow man, detective," he said, "but you got here at last. And you are a hard man to kill. The last time I saw you, you were rolling off a roof."

Stratemeyer touched the bandage still wrapped tightly around his head. He grunted. "I'll have a scar the rest of my life to remind me."

Rafe shrugged.

"What've you been doing? Housecleaning?"

"Yes, gringo. That is what I have been doing."

Stratemeyer nodded. "About what I figured."

"Have you come to take me back to Sonora?"

"I have. And to a trial. This one will be a fair trial,

Rafe. That I promise you. But I have what I need for a conviction."

"I am sure." Rafe smiled. "But you will not hang me. I will not allow that."

"I am afraid a jury will have to decide that, Rafe."

"No. I shall decide." Rafe was no longer smiling. "I am going to draw my weapon, detective. If you do not shoot me, I will shoot you and ride out of here." He patted the saddlebags draped over the horse's pommel. "And I will ride out a wealthy man."

"That explosion I heard. Your mine?"

"Yes. As you say, I am housecleaning."

"Where's O'Hare?"

"I sent him away. Forget him. You have me to contend with. That is enough."

"Come back with me, Rafe. I don't want to kill you."

"I am counting on that," Rafe said, drawing his revolver.

Stratemeyer aimed at the man's narrow chest and fired. The round caught Rafe just below the breast pocket of his jacket, knocking him to the ground. But he was not dead. Not yet. Pushing himself up to a sitting position, Rafe doggedly brought his weapon up a second time. Swiftly, Stratemeyer fired again, stamping a neat hole in the man's white shirt. Dropping his weapon, Rafe fell backward into the grass. His horse wheeled and galloped a short distance, then pulled up, its reins dragging.

Stratemeyer approached Rafe cautiously, kicked the man's weapon away, and knelt down to him. A quick inspection of his wounds convinced Stratemeyer that the outlaw was near death.

"Dammit, Rafe! That was a fool move!"

"Do not let it bother you," Rafe said, his voice very faint. "I have been dead since they hung my Josita. Now it only remains for me to complete the journey." He smiled, a ghastly twisted smile. "But I have avenged her death—almost."

"You thinking of Bill Finney?"

"Yes."

"I think you should know, Rafe. He was sorry for his part in Josita's hanging."

"You say, 'was'?"

Stratemeyer nodded grimly. "He shot himself last night."

"You make a dying man happy, amigo. Thank you for telling me this." The smile faded from Rafe's face. "Now, listen. There is an empty grave on the slope above the cabin. Bury me there and you can keep the gold in my saddlebags."

"I don't want your gold, but I'll bury you there if you want."

Rafe looked into Stratemeyer's eyes for a moment longer, as if trying to measure this particular gringo's honesty. Then, apparently satisfied, he closed his eyes. His head dropped back into the grass. A barely perceptible tremor passed through his slight frame, and then he was still.

Stratemeyer stood up. He wondered for a moment why he had told Rafael Escobar about Bill Finney; then he shrugged and went after Rafe's horse. He had not lied when he told Rafe he did not want his gold. He would bury it with him.

Remembering the greedy glint in Sharon Cortland's lovely eyes, he shuddered. This gold had a stink to it.

Chapter 14

As Manders sat at the table, fidgeting with a menu, he found himself at a loss for words. Maud's company never had been comfortable, and here in Sonora it was nearly unbearable. He looked up nervously, hoping the head-waiter would remember his instructions.

As soon as Belle appeared in the dining room doorway, she was led immediately to their table. At her approach, Manders got quickly to his feet, introduced Belle to his wife, and then seated her. He did this last with elaborate courtesy and obvious affection.

As he had intended, none of this was lost on his wife.

"Belle, is it?" Maud asked, her voice so powerful a few heads at nearby tables turned suddenly in Maud's direction.

"Yes. Belle Harper."

"And where are you from?"

Belle smiled. "It is not where I am from, but where I am going that matters."

Maud pulled herself to her full height and stared coldly at her husband. "A creature without manners," she commented, as if Belle were no longer present. "I can understand the attraction for both of you."

174

"Confound it, Maud," Manders said, his voice soft but powerful. "That remark was uncalled for."

Despite herself, Belle felt perspiration beginning to trickle down her neck. Manders had done his best to prepare her for Maud, but it had been a task beyond his talents.

Maud was not a woman at all. She was a creature out of some fearsome myth. As hefty as a stevedore, she had the cold, unblinking eyes of a bird of prey, hair on her upper lip, and a voice that rivaled in carrying power that of a foghorn. She wore her hair piled on top of her head in an untidy bun, and her gray, heavily beaded dress was a featureless though obviously expensive sack that did absolutely nothing for her. She did not use rouge or lipstick, and her round face had the flaccid consistency of bread dough.

Belle could see that Maud distressed Ted. She terrified Belle.

They ordered. No one else in the restaurant could possibly have been unaware of Maud's judicious and lengthy selections from the elaborate menu. Later, while Manders and Belle ate in a heavy, dismayed silence, Maud consumed her four courses in a snuffling, head-bobbing rush.

Afterward, with undiminished gusto, she gulped down two large glasses of the wine she had ordered; then she turned her piratical eyes on Belle and her husband.

"I don't believe in beating around the bush," she proclaimed to the universe at large. "I hate this country. It is wild . . . uncivilized. If it is a divorce you want, Theodore, you shall have it. All I want is a fair share of your earnings."

"How much," Manders asked softly, in a desperate effort to get Maud to keep her voice down as well, "do you consider a fair share?"

"Half, at least."

Manders swallowed and looked at Belle, who smiled encouragingly at him. Manders looked back at Maud.

"Done."

"Then we shall visit your bank tomorrow. I have already obtained the services of a lawyer."

"As you wish."

Maud stood up. "I am going to my room. Alone."

Manders got hastily to his feet, but Maud swept heedlessly past him and disappeared from the dining room. Almost at once, it seemed to Belle, the place got larger, more spacious.

Manders sat down and summoned a waiter.

"Champagne," he told him. "Chilled."

"She is going to be very surprised when she discovers she is getting half of nothing," Belle said. "I would not want to be there."

"I can handle it. I think."

Belle reached over and took his hand. With a wry smile, she said, "Be brave."

He smiled back at her. "I can afford to be now. Today I paid off my foreman and all the workers. At both diggings. I had enough money for that, at least."

"Tell me, Ted," Belle said, as the waiter brought them their champagne and began to pour. "All that money you sent her. What did she do—eat it?"

"I believe so. But I really don't have the faintest idea. I think she has some relatives in Philadelphia who are investing heavily in a three-wheeled carriage of some kind. From what I gather, the horse is hitched to the rear. It's all very complicated, I understand. They have great hopes for it."

"That's where most of the money went?"

"I have a pretty good idea that's where it is going. Yes."

"So in a couple of days Maud will get fifty percent of nothing. And the world will never get to ride in a three-wheeled carriage with the horse in the rear."

"Now, isn't that a damn shame?" Manders asked, a happy grin on his face.

Laughing with him, Belle took up her champagne and the two clinked their glasses in salute.

As they downed the champagne, a sudden burst of

applause came from all around them. Startled, Belle glanced about and saw a room full of smiling faces, each one nodding approval. Many of them Belle and Manders had come to know in the short week since they had met. The rest evidently had enough sense to realize what it was they had just witnessed.

Manders waved the waiter over and ordered champagne for all the other diners.

"Can you afford it?" Belle whispered in some dismay.

"Of course I can. Or would you rather I save it for Maud?"

Belle shook her head decisively. Manders reached into the bucket for the champagne bottle and filled their glasses to the brim.

Sharon and Dan Prentiss had learned of Rafe Barnett's death and Brett O'Hare's disappearance as soon as they had returned to Sonora from honeymooning in San Francisco. At once they purchased a wagon and supplies and hurried out to the valley, assuming they now were the sole owners of Rafe Barnett's secret gold mine. As the detective from Chicago had remarked, they had their own Ali Baba's cave. But now they were not so sure.

Sharon got down from the wagon, stunned. A much healthier Dan Prentiss hopped down beside her.

"I'm *sure* this is the valley," she said.

"I know it is," insisted Dan. "There's the creek. Those mountain flanks are the same."

Shading her eyes, Sharon said, "I see it! The cabin. But it has burned to the ground!"

Looking up at the mountain's towering flanks, Dan asked, "Where's that boulder?"

"Could that be it?" Sharon asked. "Over there?"

"Where?"

"On the far side of the creek—against that knoll."

Squinting through the sunlight, Dan studied it for a moment. It certainly did not look as if it belonged there. "I suppose that could be it. Must have rolled down off the slope."

"What could have caused that? An earthquake, do you think?"

Dan shrugged. "Maybe."

"Dan, how are we going to find the mine?"

"Don't worry, Sharon. We'll find it, all right."

They clambered back up into their wagon. Dan set the team in motion, and they drove on into the valley. When they reached the burned-out cabin, they got down from the wagon and gazed up at the forested slopes that loomed above them. The closer they got to these vaulting, intimidating flanks of timber and stone, the more unsure they became of just where to begin their search for the mine entrance. It was strange how much they had relied on that boulder as a marker and how completely unfamiliar the mountainside looked without it.

Undaunted, they set off into the timber and a moment later were struggling up the steep slope.

It was late in the afternoon. Sharon and Dan, footsore and weary, were perched on a small, grassy shelf overlooking the valley. The cabin and their wagon were out of sight behind a stand of pine. For most of that afternoon, they had tramped up one slope and down another, at one time coming upon what appeared to be two fresh graves. Gulleys had yawned before them, and abrupt cliffs had barred their progress. Twice they thought they had found the correct path leading to the mine entrance, only to be led still higher into the mountains.

The entrance to the mine had vanished.

"You're right, Sharon," Dan said wearily. "It must have been an earthquake. Remember that tremor in San Francisco?"

She shuddered. "It was terrifying."

"The mine is gone—as if the mountain just swallowed it up. My God, Sharon. I don't think we'll ever find it."

"I know. That's what I've been thinking, too."

"What are we going to do?"

Sharon looked at Dan. "Does it make all that much difference?"

"What do you mean? Of course, it does! We could be rich!"

"But we *are* rich," she said softly. "Look around at this valley. Isn't it beautiful? Smell the pines and listen to the birds. Dan, this valley is the real gold of California. Can you imagine what would happen if word got out that we had a gold mine here? Think of what that stream would look like in just a few days. And the tents and shacks everywhere. The smell. The sickness."

"I know, Sharon. You're right. But all that gold! It's here somewhere. I can feel it!"

Sharon reached out and took Dan's hand. "I can feel it too, Dan. But let me tell you something. I didn't like us much while we were on our honeymoon in San Francisco." She rested her head on his shoulder. "I mean that, Dan. Not at all. Having that gold did something to me, Dan. Something to us. And I didn't like it."

Dan looked away, obviously troubled. "I could feel it, too," he admitted at last. "It was like the gold owned us, not the other way around."

"Yes! The gold was telling us what to do, making us into something we didn't want to be. Dan, listen! We still have some gold left. Let's put it aside for now and build a cabin alongside that stream." She pointed quickly. "Next to that big cottonwood. Maybe then we'll find something better and more lasting than gold."

"A home?"

"Yes, Dan."

Dan smiled. He felt as if a curse had been lifted from his soul. "Building a cabin will be hard work, Sharon—for both of us."

"I don't care."

At once they started for the valley floor. Before night fell, they had built a roaring fire at the spot where they planned to build, and the sound of Dan's ax was already echoing on the timbered slopes.

It was curiosity that brought Stratemeyer back to the valley four months later. Topping a gentle rise halfway into it, he caught sight of a recently built log cabin gleaming in the bright morning sunlight, a wagon sitting in the front yard, horses grazing in a distant meadow.

Sitting on the far side of the stream, the cabin was shaded by a large cottonwood. A fieldstone chimney was not yet completed, but a thin spiral of woodsmoke was coming from a stovepipe thrust through a window. It was a good, warm, welcoming smell.

As the detective rode closer, Dan Prentiss emerged from the house with Sharon beside him. Stratemeyer waved to them. They shaded their eyes to see who it was, then, waving excitedly, began running across the grass to meet him.

Dismounting a moment later, Stratemeyer shook their hands heartily. He was delighted with how well they looked. They seemed positively glowing with happiness and were obviously very glad to see him.

"Got some trouble to clear up in Oregon Territory," Stratemeyer told them. "Heard in Sonora you'd come back from San Francisco and bought a wagon and headed north. Thought I'd go this way to see how you were doing." He looked around. "Funny. Don't see no diggings."

"And no sign of a gold mine, either," said Dan, smiling.

"We just couldn't find it!" said Sharon helplessly, her face glowing.

"Well, maybe it's for the best. You two sure look happy enough."

"We are, Mr. Stratemeyer." Sharon took Dan's arm and for a moment the two beamed at each other. Then Sharon broke the spell, remembering their guest.

"There's fresh coffee on. You must come in and set a spell and tell us the news."

"Much obliged," the big detective said. "I'd sure appreciate the coffee. I got a ways to go yet before sundown, so I'll just stay long enough to give you the news."

"Then tell me about Belle Harper! Do you remember her?"

"Of course."

"How is she? She was so kind to me."

"She's Mrs. Belle Manders now. She left Sonora with Manders in a wagon and a fresh span of mules a few days before I left. Seems some friends of Manders need his engineering skill to reach a deep vein of gold-bearing quartz in the mountains southeast of here. The two of them seemed quite happy, as a matter of fact."

Sharon took a deep breath, obviously relieved. "I'm so glad to hear that. The last time I spoke to Belle she was a little worried."

Dan laughed. "And I don't wonder. I got a look at that woman Manders left behind. She reminded me of a grizzly."

Sharon turned on her husband. "Now, Dan! That's not fair."

"That's right," drawled Stratemeyer. "Ain't fair to the grizzlies."

In spite of herself, Sharon smiled, and the three of them were still chuckling a moment later when they reached the cabin.

It was close to noon when Stratemeyer left. He had enjoyed his visit too much to cut it short and did not regret the delay. As he waved good-bye to them and rode on through the valley, he felt a warm glow. He would likely never see Sharon or Dan again, but no longer would he worry about them and their greed for gold.

The sickness had passed them by. He had been tempted to tell them of the gold he had buried under Rafael Escobar, but only for a moment. Let Rafael Escobar's bones lie undisturbed—his gold with him.

Sharon and Dan Prentiss had found a far richer harvest in this sweet valley.

Coming in February 1984 . . .

STAGECOACH STATION 10:
ABILENE
by Hank Mitchum

"Hell is in session!"—that's what they said about the end-of-the-world cattle town of Abilene, Kansas. Vice and violence are so wild and widespread that town officials are forced to hire men either brave or foolhardy enough to put a lid on this seething cauldron.

One of those men is James Butler "Wild Bill" Hickok.

Soon a stagecoach arrives bearing six passengers whose lives will become fatefully intertwined with that of the already-legendary gunman: Elliot Carson, the new editor of the *Abilene Chronicle*; Connie Witherspoon, a beautiful brunette whose skill with words quickly makes her the voice of the women of Abilene; Mike Williams, an idealistic young man who yearns to become Wild Bill's deputy; Sue Ann Mobley, a tragic young woman whose dream of a life in the theater is shattered by the realities of an untamed cow town; Agnes Lake Thatcher, a strong-willed older woman who will not be denied her own dream of marrying Wild Bill; and Jim Mulrey, a dangerous drifter with a grudge that can only be satisfied by Hickok's death.

As they step from the stage, they will find their destiny—be it love, or death—waiting on the streets of Abilene.

Read ABILENE, on sale February 1984 wherever Bantam paperbacks are sold.

★ WAGONS WEST ★

A series of unforgettable books that trace the lives of a dauntless band of pioneering men, women, and children as they brave the hazards of an untamed land in their trek across America. This legendary caravan of people forge a new link in the wilderness. They are Americans from the North and the South, alongside immigrants, Blacks, and Indians, who wage fierce daily battles for survival on this uncompromising journey—each to their private destinies as they fulfill their greatest dreams.

☐	22808	INDEPENDENCE!	$3.50
☐	22784	NEBRASKA!	$3.50
☐	23177	WYOMING!	$3.50
☐	22568	OREGON!	$3.50
☐	23168	TEXAS!	$3.50
☐	23381	CALIFORNIA!	$3.50
☐	23405	COLORADO!	$3.50
☐	20174	NEVADA!	$3.50
☐	20919	WASHINGTON!	$3.50
☐	22925	MONTANA!	$3.95
☐	23572	DAKOTA!	$3.95

Prices and availability subject to change without notice.

Buy them at your local bookstore or use this handy coupon:

**FROM THE PRODUCER OF WAGONS WEST
AND THE KENT FAMILY CHRONICLES—
A SWEEPING SAGA OF WAR AND HEROISM
AT THE BIRTH OF A NATION.**

THE WHITE INDIAN SERIES

Filled with the glory and adventure of the colonization of America, here is the thrilling saga of the new frontier's boldest hero and his family. Renno, born to white parents but raised by Seneca Indians, becomes a leader in both worlds. THE WHITE INDIAN SERIES chronicles the adventures of Renno, his son Ja-gonh, and his grandson Ghonkaba, from the colonies to Canada, from the South to the turbulent West. Through their struggles to tame a savage continent and their encounters with the powerful men and passionate women in the early battles for America, we witness the events that shaped our future and forged our great heritage.

☐	22714	White Indian #1	$3.50
☐	22715	The Renegade #2	$3.50
☐	22716	War Chief #3	$3.50
☐	22717	The Sachem #4	$3.50
☐	22718	Renno #5	$3.50
☐	20559	Tomahawk #6	$3.50
☐	23022	War Cry #7	$3.50
☐	23576	Ambush #8	$3.50

Prices and availability subject to change without notice.

SPECIAL
MONEY SAVING
OFFER

Now you can have an up-to-date listing of Bantam's hundreds of titles plus take advantage of our unique and exciting bonus book offer. A special offer which gives you the opportunity to purchase a Bantam book for only 50¢. Here's how!

By ordering any five books at the regular price per order, you can also choose any other single book in the catalog (up to a $4.95 value) for just 50¢. Some restrictions do apply, but for further details why not send for Bantam's illustrated Shop-At-Home Catalog today!

Just send us your name and address plus 50¢ to defray the postage and handling costs.